# ROAD TRIPPED

This book belongs to

**Thomas**

# Also by Pete Hautman

*The Flinkwater Factor*

*The Forgetting Machine*

*Blank Confession*

*All-In*

*Rash*

*Invisible*

*Godless* (Winner of the National Book Award)

*Sweetblood*

*No Limit*

*Mr. Was*

# PETE HAUTMAN

SIMON & SCHUSTER BFYR

New York   London   Toronto   Sydney   New Delhi

SIMON & SCHUSTER BFYR

An imprint of Simon & Schuster Children's Publishing Division

1230 Avenue of the Americas, New York, New York 10020

This book is a work of fiction. Any references to historical events, real people, or real places are used fictitiously. Other names, characters, places, and events are products of the author's imagination, and any resemblance to actual events or places or persons, living or dead, is entirely coincidental.

For information about special discounts for bulk purchases, please contact Simon & Schuster Special Sales at 1-866-506-1949 or business@simonandschuster.com.

The Simon & Schuster Speakers Bureau can bring authors to your live event. For more information or to book an event, contact the Simon & Schuster Speakers Bureau at 1-866-248-3049 or visit our website at www.simonspeakers.com.

Also available in a SIMON & SCHUSTER BFYR hardcover edition

Book design by Tom Daly

The text for this book was set in Excelsior LT Std.

Manufactured in the United States of America

First SIMON & SCHUSTER BFYR paperback edition May 2020

10 9 8 7 6 5 4 3 2 1

The Library of Congress has cataloged the hardcover edition as follows:

Names: Hautman, Pete, 1952– author.

Title: Road tripped / Pete Hautman.

Description: First edition. | New York : Simon & Schuster Books for Young Readers, [2019] | Summary: Seventeen-year-old Steven "Stiggy" Gabel tries to cope with his father's suicide, his mother's depression, and his girlfriend's departure by taking off down the Great River Road from Minnesota to Louisiana.

Identifiers: LCCN 2018030155| ISBN 9781534405905 (hc) ] | ISBN 9781534405912 (pbk) | ISBN 9781534405929 (eBook)

Subjects: | CYAC: Coming of age—Fiction. | Automobile travel—Fiction. | Interpersonal relations—Fiction. | Runaways—Fiction. | Mississippi River Region—Fiction.

Classification: LCC PZ7.H2887 Ro 2019 | DDC [Fic]—dc23

LC record available at https://lccn.loc.gov/2018030155

Everybody goes home in October.

—Jack Kerouac, *On the Road*

# "Walking in London"
## Concrete Blonde
## 6:49

**I go west, I go south, I go east, I go out of the** suburbs, out of my life. I have no destination, but with every mile the bindings stretch, become thin. I turn left, I turn right, I pass a Fleet Farm, a Walmart, truck stops, cornfields, dead deer by the side of the road.

I roll through Red Wing and take the arching bridge up and out of Minnesota, over the Mississippi River, across the flat causeway spanning the Wisconsin Channel. The bluffs ahead are ablaze with red, orange, and yellow. I am blazing too.

My phone chimes. A text. I look at it. It's my mom. I lower the window and sail the phone out over the embankment, into the river. A cord snaps, my heart thrums, my blood fizzes, my arms and legs seem to stretch, my hair is alive.

Then I remember that all my music is on my phone. Well, shit.

It doesn't matter.

I am not thinking about Garf, I am not thinking about Gaia, I am not thinking about my father.

I'm gone.


I set the cruise control and tip my seat back so my fingers barely reach the bottom of the wheel. I pretend I've got a trunk full of hundred-dollar bills, instead of $407 in cash and my mom's Visa card. She'll probably cancel it when she realizes it's gone.

To my right, the Mississippi River flows sluggish and murky; tree-covered bluffs tower above on the left. I imagine a beautiful girl standing on the shoulder next to her broken-down car.

*Hop in,* I say, and she does.

*Nice wheels,* she says. *What is this, a Camaro?*

*Mustang,* I say.

She's wearing a black T-shirt, and she has black hair. That makes me think of Gaia, so I change her T-shirt to red and her hair to blond. I change my dirt-colored hair to blond, so now we match.

*Where to?* I ask my imaginary passenger.

*Same as you,* she says. *Nowhere.*

She's already boring, so I stop imagining the girl

and just watch the scenery slide by and don't think about Gaia.

Every few miles I have to slow down for some little town. Bay City. Maiden Rock. Stockholm. I guess there are towns like that all up and down the river, beads on a wet muddy chain. I suppose people have to live someplace—I mean, I grew up in Saint Andrew Valley, just another crappy little suburb.

Pepin. Nelson. Alma. I'm getting hungry and the Mustang is getting thirsty, so I stop at a Kwik Trip. I use my mom's Visa card to fill the tank, then go inside and grab a microwave burrito and a Dew. While the burrito is heating up, I look at a spinner rack of caps. Most of them are Green Bay Packers caps, but I find one with a John Deere logo. I like the way it looks, and it feels ironic: *Dear John*, only backward.

"What are all those signs I see?" I ask the guy behind the counter as he rings up my purchases. "The ones that say 'Great River Road.'"

"You're on it." He gestures proudly at the highway, as if he built it himself. "The Great River Road."

"What's so great about it?"

His smile fades a bit. "It's just what they call it."

"So it goes all the way down to the Gulf of Mexico?"

"There're a few twists and turns—it goes on both sides of the river—but yeah, I guess you could take it to the gulf. Never driven it myself. There's a map on the freebie rack." He points at a wire stand with all sorts of tourist info.

I grab a Great River Road map and a few random brochures on my way out.

Back in the Mustang, still sitting at the gas pump, I unwrap the burrito and take a bite. It could've used another twenty seconds in the microwave. I open the map and spread it across the steering wheel. There are dozens of red triangles marking "points of interest" along the river, all the way from northern Minnesota to Louisiana. I take another bite and chew slowly as I find Alma on the map. I follow the highway south with my eyes until I get to Prairie du Chien, Wisconsin. I close my eyes.

Just seeing the words "Prairie du Chien" makes me want to puke. I crumple the map with one hand and throw it into the backseat. I can hear myself breathing. *Prairie du Chien. Gaia.* I'm not going there. No way am I going there.

I shove the rest of the burrito into my mouth. It's too much. I have to force swallow and wash it down with half the bottle of Dew.

A car horn blasts. A guy in the pickup truck behind me wants to pull up to the pump. The half-chewed burrito is still slowly descending my esophagus. I look back and give him the finger. He gets out of his truck, and he's *huge.* I start the car and screech out of the gas station. For the next couple miles I keep checking my rearview, expecting to see the big grill of the pickup bearing down on me, but I guess I'm not worth the trouble.

Twenty minutes later I hit Fountain City. I cross a bridge back to the Minnesota side and continue south, now with the river between me and Prairie du Chien.

Not thinking about Gaia, not thinking about Garf, not thinking about my dad.

Instead, I'm thinking about the moonfaced cop.

# Happy Birthday

**The cop thing happened weeks ago, but it** feels like yesterday. I had talked my mom into letting me drive to school because it was the first day, and it was my birthday. I wanted to take Dad's Mustang, but she wouldn't let me.

"Why not?" I said. "It's just sitting in the garage!"

"You know why," she said. "Take my car."

Her car was a Toyota Corolla, but whatever. Better than the bus.

On the way to school I got stuck behind this minivan doing twenty-five in a thirty. I figured it was some lady texting. I gave her a blast with my horn. She slowed down even more. I pulled into the opposite lane and floored it. As I passed, I looked over and saw it wasn't a woman; it was a guy with a big white face like the moon. I showed him my middle finger as I passed. What a jerk. I swerved back in front of him and slowed way down for a minute just to give him a taste of his own jerkiness.

I got to school a few minutes early. My plan was to intercept Gaia as she got off her bus and talk her into skipping the first day of school. We could drive around and do whatever we wanted because it was my birthday, and I had a car, and it would be fun. But things didn't work out the way I'd planned.

I don't want to think about it.

Anyway, later that same day, in the afternoon, I was driving down Flagg Avenue making a mental list of all the assholes I'd run into recently. There were a lot of them. I figured I must be an asshole magnet. Like, I was giving off some sort of radiation that attracted them. Because I kept running into way more than my share.

That was when I saw the lights flashing in my rear-view.

The cop had thirty pounds of junk on his belt, and a pair of mirrored aviators he probably thought made him look badass. They didn't.

"Do you know why I pulled you over?" he asked.

"Not really," I said. I'd been going maybe five miles over the limit. They don't usually pull you over for that. I thought maybe I had a taillight out.

"Let's have a look at your license."

I handed him my driver's license.

He read my name to me out loud, as if I didn't know it. "Steven Gerald Gabel. Born seventeen years ago today. How come you're not in school, Steven?"

"I dropped out." I hadn't, but I was thinking about it.

"Why would you do that?"

*Why is he giving me a hard time?* I wondered.

"Calculus," I said. "It's bullshit."

"Is that a fact?" Like he had any idea what I was talking about. "Don't go anywhere." He took my license back to his car to run me through his computer. I knew what he'd find—a speeding ticket from April, and maybe that thing that had happened at Wigglesworth's, which wasn't my fault. I watched him in my side mirror, sitting in his copmobile. I was a little nervous because maybe he'd find something I'd done that I'd forgotten about, but mostly I was just pissed off about the whole thing and feeling trapped because I knew I'd have to just sit there not saying what I was really thinking, or he'd write me up.

Finally he came waddling back, all his cop junk slowing him down.

"Do you know why I pulled you over?" he asked.

*Oh, so we're playing this game now.*

"You already asked me that," I said. "No idea."

"A citizen complaint, *Stiggy*. You were driving erratically, speeding, and making obscene gestures. You know anything about that?"

"When was this?"

*And how does he know to call me Stiggy?*

"Seven twenty-seven this morning, on Trident Avenue."

"Oh." I was a bit startled by the precision of his response. "So I flip a guy off, and he SWATs me?"

The cop took off his aviators and regarded me with a flat smile, his big round face pinking with triumph, and I recognized him.

"You were the guy in the minivan," I said to the moonfaced cop.

"That's right. I was on my way to work. Didn't expect to see *you* again so soon."

I figured it was time to shut up, so I did. He leaned in so close I could smell the triple bacon cheeseburger he'd had for lunch. "I could tag you for reckless driving, *Stiggy*. You passed me going forty-five or fifty. But I'm not gonna do that, *Stiggy*. You know why?"

"No idea."

"Because it's your birthday. And because I used to be a little pissant like you, and look how I turned out."

It was all I could do to not say, *You grew up to be an asshole cop?*

"So I'm giving you a break," he said. "But I want you to take it easy, *Stiggy*."

I had to ask. "How do you know to call me Stiggy?"

*Is he smiling?* I wondered. *I think he's smiling.*

"Seriously," I said.

He said, "Remember Old Navy?"

Oh, shit. I'd forgot about that.


It was all my mom's fault. Last year she bought me a hoodie from Old Navy for my birthday.

"All the kids are wearing Old Navy clothes," she said. "I knew you'd like it."

*Like it?* Well, I didn't *hate* it, but when I put it on, my wrists stuck six inches out of the sleeves.

"Aren't you a medium?" my mom said.

"Not at Old Navy," I said.

"Oh, well. You can exchange it," she said cheerfully.

So that's what I did. Except when I got to Old Navy, all the clerks were really busy and I didn't feel like waiting in line, so I went to the hoodie display and swapped the medium for an extra large, and as I was walking out, this mall cop with a big stupid-looking mustache grabbed me and accused me of shoplifting. I tried to explain, and I showed him the receipt, but he was having none of it.

"What's your name, son?" he asked.

"Justin Bieber," I told him.

"Okay, have it your way." He hauled me over to security and told me I was going to stay there until I gave him my real name and my parent's phone number.

"This is kidnapping," I said.

"You want me to call the cops, *Justin*?" he said.

"My name's Stiggy," I said.

"Stiggy? What's that, your *street* name?"

*What an idiot.*

"It's a *nick*name," I said.

"How about a real name?"

"How about you kiss my ass?"

I probably shouldn't have said that, because that's when he decided to "make an example" of me. He called the cops, and they hauled me to the station. It must have been a slow day. They booked me, the whole routine with fingerprints and my real name: Steven Gerald Gabel, aka "Stiggy." What a joke.

Mom was great when she showed up. She gave the cops a piece of her mind, telling them I didn't steal anything, that I was just exchanging a shirt. They didn't believe me, but they believed her. I think they were a little embarrassed by the whole thing—but not embarrassed enough to tear up my arrest record.

"That was bullshit," I said to the moonfaced cop. "I was never charged with anything."

"Yeah, well, you have a record," said the cop. "Listen, Stiggy, you want some advice?"

I didn't, but I just shrugged.

"Okay, here it is. Don't be such a dick. Your life will improve."

I wanted to say, *Why don't you learn how to drive? Maybe you're the dick.*

"My life is fine," I said.

"You're seventeen, you're not in school, and you're flipping off strangers on the road. I don't call that *fine*."

"Yeah, well, maybe you deserved to get flipped off," I muttered. I couldn't help it.

Unfortunately, the cop had good ears. He stared at me for a few seconds, then said, "You know what? I lied about not tagging you."

He gave me a ticket for speeding and illegal passing.

"Happy birthday, *Stiggy*."

# "21st Century Schizoid Man"
## King Crimson
## 3:32

**Turns out the Great River Road is a total** crock.

In the first place, it's not just one road; it's, like, a hundred different roads that sorta-kinda follow the Mississippi on both sides, and if you happen to miss a sign, you can get completely lost. Even if you manage to stay on the right road, most of the time you can't see the river. It might be a mile away, or ten miles—there's no way to tell. The road zigs and zags and shudders and twists through all these little towns, most of which look half-abandoned. This one town I went through, the biggest building has a sign that reads UNDERTAKER • FURNITURE • CARPETING. Like the owner couldn't decide.

That was an hour ago. Now I am hopelessly lost on
a dirt road that apparently leads nowhere. I think I'm
going south, but it's cloudy and I can't tell for sure.
Being lost on a dirt road makes me think of Gaia
again. I pull off to the side and grab the crumpled
map from the backseat. It's no help—this is the sort
of map that shows only the places it wants you to go,
not the roads where you're totally lost. I rummage
through the glove compartment, thinking maybe
there's a real map in there. I find no map, but I do
find my dad's iPod. I'd forgotten all about that. I try
to turn it on. Nothing. It's dead. Duh. It's been dead
ever since Gaia found it under the seat, and that was
three months ago.

I keep digging, and find a charging cord. There's a
USB port inside the console. I plug in the iPod. A second later the screen lights up. I wonder what I'll find
in there. I keep driving and let it charge.

A few minutes later I come into a small town.
Really small. A café that's been closed for years, a
couple churches, and an old-fashioned service station. My gauge is on empty, so I pull in. It's not the
sort of place I'd normally go on purpose. There are
only two pumps. When I get out of the car, I see that
there is no credit card reader. Every other gas station
I've been in, I just swipe my mom's credit card to pay.
I figure I should use the credit card as much as possible before she cancels it.

I'm standing there looking confused when this

greasy old dude comes limping out, wiping his hands on an even greasier rag.

"Hep ya?" he says.

"Um . . . do you take credit cards?"

"Sure do. Fill 'er up?"

I nod. The man twists off the gas cap and shoves in the pump nozzle.

"Check the oil?" he asks.

"No, I think it's okay."

"Suit yerself." He unhooks a spray bottle from his belt and starts spraying the windows and wiping them down with the gray rag. He does a good job, making sure to clean the glass right to the edges. It's weird. I never had anybody do that before.

The pump clicks off. He hangs the nozzle back on the pump and screws the gas cap back on. I hand him the credit card. He takes it back into the office. A minute later he comes back outside and holds out a sort of tablet with a strip of paper clipped to it. He hands me a pen.

"Need your John Henry," he says.

"It's John Hancock," I say. "Not 'Henry.'"

One of Dad's pet peeves was people saying things wrong. Like, if somebody said the word "irregardless," he would correct them on the spot. *That's not a word,* he would say. *It's just "regardless."* Mom would roll her eyes and look away.

"'Hancock,' eh?" says the old man. "Whadya know! Always thought it was 'Henry.'" He does not seem to be offended. He reminds me of Garf, if Garf were sixty years old. I could say anything to Garf. Well, almost anything.

I sign the slip. He tears off the top copy and gives it to me. "All set," he says.

I get back into the Mustang, hoping to find my way back to the twenty-first century, thinking about Garf Neff.

# Garf

**After my birthday encounter with the moon-**faced cop, I stopped in at Brain Food Comics and Collectibles. I found Garf flipping through the used comics, something he did most days after school.

Garf's real name was "Garfield," but everybody called him Garf.

Tobias was watching him from behind the counter, hoping for an excuse to kick him out, because Garf hardly ever bought anything.

"Where were you today?" Garf asked me. "I didn't see you in school."

"Getting a ticket," I said. "Do you believe in asshole magnetism?"

"You mean *animal* magnetism?"

"If I'd *meant* 'animal,' I'd have *said* 'animal.'"

"Oh. In that case I got no idea what you're talking about."

I explained my theory to him. One thing about Garf, he'd listen to ten kinds of crazy without blinking.

"Maybe it's like a psychic power," he said. "Like, you expect people to act a certain way, and they pick up on your brain waves."

"You mean if I think some guy is going to be a jerk, then he decides to be a jerk just for me? I turn him into a jerk with my mental powers?"

"Something like that."

"That's the stupidest thing I ever heard."

"No stupider than what you said." Garf and I were always calling each other stupid.

"Whatever. I seem to attract more than my share. Like that dick Nestor."

"Who's Nestor?"

"Calculus. He tried to confiscate my phone this morning."

"Why?"

"Because he's a dick. All I did was check for a text."

"You're not supposed to do that," Garf said, not looking at me, still flipping through the bin of comics.

"Yeah, well, I walked out."

"You walked out?"

"What did I just say?" Garf could be kind of slow.

"You said you walked out."

"I took off."

"You just left? On the first day of school?"

"Yeah. I'm done."

Now Garf looked at me, tipping his head to the side like he thought he was being shined. "You serious?"

"I'm done with calculus, anyway. I don't need it to graduate."

"Oh! I thought you meant you were dropping out."

"I'm thinking about that, too."

"What about Gaia?" he asked. "I didn't see her today either."

"Don't talk to me about Gaia."

He gave me this Garf look. "Okaaay . . . ?" he said, dragging it out and putting a question mark at the end.

I turned my back and walked out of the store.

# "Kiss Them for Me"

## Siouxsie & the Banshees
### 4:39

**I am lost in Iowa and it's after midnight. I** haven't seen the so-called Great River Road in hours of driving. The roads have weird names like C7X and XC3, which is not helpful, and the main attraction is a roadkill raccoon every half mile or so. I know I should stop and ask somebody for directions, but then I think about my dad, who would never do that because he would never admit he was lost. We always found our way home eventually.

The only thing that's keeping me awake is the music. Dad's iPod is full of the weirdest collection of tunes I've ever heard. Nine hundred songs, everything from the B-52s to Beethoven. I never knew. He never listened to music at home. We never talked about music, except when he'd ask me to turn down whatever I had blasting in my room. I figured he hated rap and hip-hop and everything else I listened to, but on his iPod I find 50 Cent, Kanye, Dre, and Snoop Dogg. The Sex Pistols and the Pixies. Nirvana and Babymetal. *Babymetal?* Dad listened to *Babymetal?*

Of course, most of it is really ancient stuff: the Beatles, the Stones, Buddy Holly, and a ton of stuff I've never heard of. Eddie Cochran? Wanda Jackson? Lesley Gore?

I set the iPod to shuffle. Rihanna puts the sub-woofer to the test as I roll through a tiny town called Elkport where nothing is open. I can barely keep my eyes open. I figure I can use Mom's credit card and stay wherever I want, but first I have to find a motel, and I'm not having any luck with that, so I pull into a rest stop in the middle of nowhere—two trees, a picnic table, and a trash can. I park next to the picnic table, turn off the car, and crank the seat back as far as it will go, close my eyes, and sink into something that resembles sleep but isn't really, because Gaia invades my thoughts like a dark angel. I try to push her aside, but every time I do, she comes back at me from another direction.

# Gaia

**I got to know Gaia Nygren in May, at the end** of my junior year.

Gaia was a year behind me in school, in tenth grade. I'd known who she was from way back in middle school—I'd seen her hanging around the edges of things—but we'd never actually talked. Her older brother Derek was a senior. Every school has a Derek—the guy who gets straight As and gets elected class president, which makes him kind of a dick by definition. Gaia was his quiet little sister who nobody paid much attention to. I didn't even know her name back then. Everybody just called her "Derek's sister."

That didn't last. When she started tenth grade, she showed up with her hair dyed black, a stud in her left nostril, lots of eyeliner, and all-black clothes. Another baby Goth, I figured. She wasn't exactly on my radar, but you couldn't help noticing her.

The first time I ever really talked to her, I had skipped American history—a crock, my dad would've said—and walked over to the McDonald's across the street from the high school. Gaia was sitting in a booth by herself picking at a red cardboard container of fries. I bought a double cheeseburger and a Coke and slid into the seat across from her. I sort of surprised myself. It was a bold move.

She regarded me from beneath her mascaraed eyelashes. It was as if she was wearing a shell, looking at me through bulletproof glass. Her black T-shirt read, *Life Sucks and Then You Die.*

"You're Gaia, right?"

"Last time I checked," she said.

"Okay if I sit here?" I unwrapped my burger.

"No," she said.

"Why not?" I took a bite.

"Because you're eating *that.* It's gross. Do you even know what's in it?"

"Don't care." I slurped down some Coke. "You ever wear anything that's not black?"

"No."

"Didn't you used to be blond?"

She glared at me. She had a good glare.

"Do you have to dye it every day? Or is once a week enough?"

"No."

"No, what? Every day?"

"'No' as in it's none of your business. You're really rude, you know that?"

"And you're really negative," I said. That made her blink.

"No, I'm not."

"Everything you say starts with 'no.' I think you might be the most negative person in the universe. I'm Stiggy, by the way."

"I know who you are." She looked me in the eyes, just for a second, then looked away.

"So, what are you doing here?" I asked. "Aren't you supposed to be in class?"

"I got kicked out."

"What for?"

"They told me to go home and change my shirt."

"Oh." I read the words on her shirt again. "My dad would've liked that shirt."

"Your dad sounds like a piece of work."

She must have realized what she'd just said, because as soon as the words left her mouth, she sort of jerked back and her eyes went wide, then darted off to the side.

"Sorry," she said. "I forgot. I heard about your dad. Sorry."

"Life sucks and then you die, right?" I took another bite of burger.

The shell closed back over her face. "Whatever." She

examined her container of fries, selected one, and bit off the tip.

"Really sorry," she mumbled.

"Not your fault."

"I suppose you miss him."

"Mostly I'm just mad at him." I had never said that out loud before.

She nodded. "I get that."

I think that was when I started to like her.

"What was he like?" she asked.

# "Tusk"

## Fleetwood Mac
## 3:33

**I wake up to thumping right next to my head.**
Blearily I look out the window and am blinded by a
flashlight. The light is lowered. I blink away afterimages and make out a face. A cop face.

I roll down the window. The cop is an older guy,
maybe my dad's age.

He says, "How you doing?" He shines his light into
the backseat.

"I'm okay."

"Been drinking?" He has his right hand on his belt,
next to his gun.

"Nope."

"This your car?"

"Sort of," I say. "It's still in my dad's name, but he's deceased, so it's my car now."

"License?" he says.

I take out my wallet, nice and easy, and hand him my driver's license. He squints at it.

"Long ways from home."

I don't say anything. I'm trying to figure out if I've broken any laws. Is sleeping at a rest stop against the rules?

"Where you headed?"

"I'm driving down the Great River Road," I say.

"Well, you ain't on it." He looks at my license again. "Seventeen. How come you're not in school?"

"I'm taking a break," I say.

The cop is thinking. I can almost hear the gears grinding in his head.

I say, "Look, I was planning to stay with my cousin in Dubuque, but I got lost, and I was getting tired, so I figured the safe thing to do was pull over and sleep for a while."

"You got a cousin in Dubuque?"

I nod, even though it's not true.

"That's fifty miles east. How'd you wind up here?"

"Like I said, I got lost."

"Sit tight," he says.

"Yes, sir," I say. Back home I couldn't have stopped myself from being all sarcastic and mouthy, but here, in a different state, with just me and the cop in the middle of nowhere, I'm pretty nervous. I mean, he isn't being particularly scary—it's not like I'm afraid he's going to shoot me or anything, but what if he throws me in jail? I can't expect my mom to come bail me out a half hour later.

The cop takes my license back to his car. The clock on the dash reads 3:09.

At 3:31 he comes back. I think he was checking to make sure the car hasn't been reported stolen. I hope he doesn't ask me for an insurance card, because I'm not sure Mom kept the Mustang insured.

He hands me my license, and says, "You rested now?"

"I guess so."

"Good, because you can't sleep here. No overnight parking."

There are no signs or anything saying that, but I don't argue. I'm pretty sure this guy has what it takes to be a first-class asshole, so I keep my mouth shut for once.

Three thirty in the morning, and I'm back on the road, heading east toward Dubuque, where I don't have a cousin. I thought all this driving would give me time to think, but what's happening in my head is more like stirring a pot of garbage soup, around and around, like things I could've said to that cop. Some of them are pretty clever. My dad was clever. He always had some remark, no matter the occasion. Like when my uncle Donny saw that my dad had bought a Mustang, he said that my dad must be having a midlife crisis. Dad said, "Give it up, Donny. You're only half a smart-ass, and it ain't the smart half."

I guess it isn't that funny, but it was at the time.

I think about some of the other things Dad said, and stir them round and round.

# Dad

**I was eight years old the first time I realized** my dad was full of it.

We were on Gray's Bay, Lake Minnetonka, trolling for walleyes. He'd rented a little aluminum boat, and he'd fixed me up with a spinner and a minnow. We'd been out for quite a while when my rod tip doubled over and the line went zipping out of the reel.

"Set the hook, Stiggy!" he yelled.

I just held on. To his credit, Dad did not grab the rod out of my hands. I won't bore you with the whole epic battle except to say that eventually I got the fish in close to the boat and saw its sleek, green-and-yellow-spotted flank, one wild shiny eye. A northern pike, as long as my arm.

Dad leaned over the side with the net. The fish made one last desperate dive under the boat. The line scraped audibly against the keel, then went slack. I reeled in and stared at the broken, twisted end of monofilament quivering in the breeze.

"Where is he?" I asked.

"He's gone, Stiggy," Dad said.

My dad's name was Ronald. He had a brother named Donald and a sister named Veronica. It was confusing because they called one another Ronny, Donny, and Roni.

Donny and Roni came over to our house for a cookout the day after I lost the fish. Dad was telling Donny about how I'd lucked on to a big one with a little number one spinner, and a minnow no bigger than a guppy. That part was true. Donny listened with a bland, attentive expression because he was the youngest of the three siblings, and even though he probably knew that my dad was full of it, Donny didn't show it.

". . . so Stiggy reeled that monster in. And, Donny, you should've seen it. A twenty pounder if it was an ounce, as long as Stiggy is tall, I swear to God. If I'd managed to get that thing into the boat, it would've sunk us. It was humongous!"

That was when I realized my dad was full of shit. Of course, I didn't think of it in those terms—I was just a kid and hadn't learned to swear yet. But it was a big deal for me, to hear my dad being full of it, because up until that day, I'd thought he was pretty much perfect.

O O O

To be fair, according to Dad *everybody* was full of it. His favorite word was "crock." I heard it almost every day growing up. Dad would see some politician on TV, and he'd say, *What a crock*, or *That's a crock*. He never said the whole original expression—"crock of shit"—because Dad never swore when I was around. Sometimes he'd just shake his head and say, *Crock!* One word.

Dad was a world-class crock server himself. He used to come home and tell us how hard his job was. You would think it was the hardest job in the world, to hear him tell it, even though all he did was move stuff around a warehouse with a forklift.

When I was ten, they had a bring-your-kid-to-work day. They made me wear a hard hat; it was so big, I had to tip my head back to see anything. I watched Dad lift a wooden pallet of crates full of machine parts fifteen feet in the air and slide it onto a steel rack. He had an expression on his face that I'd never seen before: smiling, relaxed, and utterly focused on his task.

"That pallet weighed as much as a car," he told me, proud to be showing me what he could do.

I spent the whole day in the warehouse watching my dad move stuff from one place to another. They even gave me a job for a while, clipping plastic tags on to pallets. When it was almost quitting time, Dad wanted me to get into the forklift and drive it a few feet and make the fork go up and down, but his supervisor said no way.

"Insurance, Ronny. If anything happened, we'd all be out of a job."

"I just want him to see what it feels like to work the levers!" Dad said.

"Sorry, Ronny. Rules are rules."

After the supervisor walked off, Dad muttered, "What a crock."

Dad thought church was a crock, but Mom and I went every Sunday to Saint Mary's. I used to look forward to it—not so much because of the mass but because I got to see Cella Kimball and her ponytail. That was when I was eleven years old. I still look at girls with ponytails. I blame that on Cella, who I never once talked to and I'm certain remains, to this day, unaware of my existence.

Dad used his Sunday mornings to do yard work: mowing, raking, or shoveling snow, depending on the season. We had a big yard. When we got home from church, he would often be in the garage, fixing whatever tool had broken that day. Dad liked fixing broken things. He always let me help him. We had a little riding mower that was twenty years old, and we fixed it all the time. We put new blades on it, replaced the tires, kept it greased and cleaned. Dad said we could squeeze another twenty years out of it.

○ ○ ○

Dad always had time for me, even when he was busy with other stuff. One time he was putting in a lot of overtime at the warehouse, and Grandma had just broke her hip and had to go to a nursing home. He was coming home late every night and making lots of phone calls and filling out insurance papers. Mom told me to leave him alone, but I went and told him about some stupid thing that had happened at school—I was just a little kid back then and didn't know any better. He looked up from the papers and said, "Let's go for a walk, Stevie." That's what everybody called me back then.

It was the middle of winter and dark out, but we walked all the way to the Canton Express and ordered egg rolls to go. We ate them on the walk home. I don't know what we talked about. It didn't matter.

That first time I talked to Gaia, sitting in McDonald's watching her pick at her french fries, I told her stuff about my dad that I'd never told anybody else.

"He was an okay dad, even if he was full of it sometimes," I said.

"My dad's full of it too," she said. "But I'd miss him if he was gone."

"You want to do something sometime?" I asked.

"What does that mean?"

"I don't know. Go see a movie or something?"

"With you?"

"Yeah."

She pressed her lips together, then said, "Okay."

# "Give Me Back My Man"
## B-52s
## 3:53

**It's five in the morning by the time I get** to Dubuque, and I'm starving. I pull into an all-night diner at the edge of town, across the highway from a place called Girlz! Girlz! Girlz! with a flashing neon woman on the sign.

The diner is called Jack's Eatery. It looks like it's been here since World War II. There's a row of cracked-vinyl-upholstered booths along the window, and a counter with stools featuring the same cracked vinyl. Two old guys who look like farmers are sitting in one of the booths. A younger guy wearing an Iowa Hawkeyes cap is hunched at one end of the counter over a cup of coffee. I take a stool. Not the one farthest away from the Hawkeyes fan, but with six stools

between us so I won't have to acknowledge his existence. Behind the counter, a man with a gray buzz cut
sees me sit down and comes over with a pot of coffee.
He grabs a thick white mug on his way, and pours it
for me without even asking what I want.

"Thanks," I say. He nods sharply and puts the pot
back onto its pad.

The guy in the Hawkeyes cap watches me add
cream and four packets of sugar to my coffee.

"Swee' tooth, huh," he says. I can tell he's drunk.

"Leave the kid alone, Bubby," the counterman says.

Bubby shrugs and lets his head sink back down
between his shoulders.

"You want something to eat?" the counterman says
to me.

I look around for a menu. The man points at a
chalkboard above the coffee machine. Six items are
listed: Jack's Special, Jack's Favorite, Jack's Classic,
Jack's Lite, Jack's Big Breakfast, Jack's Gobbler.

"What is Jack's Gobbler?" I ask.

"Turkey sausage, two eggs, hash browns, and toast."

"What's the special?"

"Turkey sausage, two eggs, hash browns, and toast."

"Are they all the same thing?"

"With the lite, you only get one egg. With the big
breakfast you get three."

"Are you Jack?"

"I'm Sal. Jack's twenty years dead."

"Oh. Okay, I'll have the classic."

"How you want your eggs?"

"Scrambled."

"Wheat toast or white?"

"White."

He turns to the grill and starts doing stuff. I hear the ding of the door opening. It's a woman with big blond hair and lots of makeup. She's wearing a tight white top, even tighter jeans, and high heels.

"Morning, Terri," says Sal.

"Hey, Sal." She takes a stool in the middle, closer to me than the drunk guy. Sal pours her a coffee.

"Can I smoke?" she asks him.

Sal looks at me and raises his eyebrows.

"I don't mind," I say.

The woman takes out a pack of Marlboros and lights one up. Sal gives her a saucer to use as an ashtray. She takes a deep drag, holds it a second, then shoots the smoke out the side of her mouth.

"Thanks," she says to me. "I needed that." She takes a closer look at me. "You're just a kid," she says.

I've been trying to figure out how old she is. It's hard to tell with all the makeup, but I think she's younger than she looks. Maybe twenty or twenty-one, which isn't that much older than me.

"I'm older than I look," I say.

"Aren't we all. Hey, Sal, you got any pie left?"

"Apple okay?"

"That's all you ever have."

"Everybody likes apple pie."

"I seen your boobies," the drunk guy says.

Terri ignores him. Sal says, "Shut up, Bubby."

"Well, I have," Bubby mutters. "It ain't like I'm gonna *do* nothing."

"Damn right you're not," Terri says.

"Could if I wanted," Bubby says under his breath.

Sal hears him and says, "Take off, Bubby."

"I didn't do nothing!"

Sal leans over the counter and gets right in his face. "Out," he says.

Bubby mutters, gets unsteadily to his feet, and shuffles out the door.

Terri shakes her head and says, "Sal, if you kick out every degenerate reprobate comes in here, you won't have any customers left."

"I always got you," Sal says.

I'm surprised to hear her say "degenerate reprobate." Those aren't words I ever expected to hear from a stripper, which is what I'm guessing she is. Not that I've ever met a stripper before.

Through the window I see Bubby walking back across the road toward Girlz! Girlz! Girlz!

"Do you work over there?" I ask.

"I am an ecdysiast." She taps the ash from her cigarette. "That's a fancy word for a girl who takes her clothes off in front of guys like Bubby."

"I know," I say, although five seconds ago I didn't.

"What are you?" she asks.

"Me?" Nobody's ever asked me that before, like I

might actually be something. I must have some weird expression on my face, because she laughs. I look away, embarrassed.

"Everybody's something," she says.

"Yeah, well, I'm not."

"What are you so mad about?"

"I'm not mad."

"Could've fooled me."

Sal slides a plate with a slice of apple pie in front of her, then goes back to the grill and flips my hash browns. He has a little smile on his face, and I think maybe he's laughing at me. I stare down at the little chrome rack with the napkin dispenser and salt and pepper and cream and sugar packets and a half-empty bottle of Tabasco sauce. I don't look up until Sal delivers my Jack's Classic: eggs, a sausage patty, hash browns, and toast. I pick up the fork and start eating. All I want is to eat and get out of here fast.

"It's a lot easier just being pissed off all the time, isn't it?" Terri says. I'm not sure if she's talking to me, but I sneak a look. She's done with her pie and is smoking another cigarette. Staring right at me. "You wake up every morning, and you know how you're going to feel, like the world is out to get you and all you can do is react, and it sucks."

"What makes you think you know how I feel in the morning?"

"I'm psychic." She laughs. "Believe me, I get it. I've been pissed off my whole life. That's why I smoke these." She waves her Marlboro in front of her face, takes a drag, and lets the smoke trickle out through her nose. "It never tastes all that good, but it jolts me out of wherever I was. Changes the way I feel. Those guys across the street that were staring at my body half an hour ago were looking for jolts too. Same thing about being pissed off. You get this little hit of that good old adrenaline, a moment of distraction from the tedious business of being your own tedious self."

I'm holding my fork full of scrambled egg in front of my mouth and staring back at her like an idiot. She keeps talking.

"You know what my dad used to do? He didn't smoke, but every morning when he woke up, he'd sit up on the edge of his bed and slap himself across the face. Twice. Hard. Like, his cheeks would be bright red for half an hour after. Just to make himself feel different. He was my alarm clock. He was in the next bedroom. I'd hear it every morning at six twenty. Two slaps."

She sucks on her cigarette and tilts her head. "So what *are* you mad about? Parents don't love you? Girlfriend dump you?" She narrows her eyes, looking closely at me, then nods sharply, as if my face has answered her question.

"Told you I was psychic," she says.

"She blocked my number," I hear myself say.

"Ghosted you, huh? That's cold." Smoke jets from her nostrils. "What did you do?"

"Nothing!"

She nods, stubs out her cigarette, puts a ten on the counter, and slides off the stool.

"Thanks, Sal."

"Later, Terri."

She takes one last narrow-eyed look at me.

"You must have done something."

# Groundhog Day

**Dad died on a Thursday morning in February.**
Groundhog Day. Mom told me he'd had an accident
at the warehouse where he worked. I didn't find out
the truth until about ten days later, when Garf Neff
told me.

Garf was not my friend at the time, but I'd known
him since the fifth grade. He was a quiet kid, not
somebody you'd pay much attention to. All I knew
about him then was he had the pointiest nose of anyone I'd ever met, and that his older brother, Jimmy,
had died the year before at college. There was a
rumor that Jimmy Neff had drunk an entire bottle of
vodka and died from alcohol poisoning, and another
rumor that he had ODed on drugs, and another

rumor that he had fallen out of his dormitory window. I didn't know then which was true—could've been all three—but I didn't really care, because, like I say, Garf wasn't my friend then, and I'd never met his brother.

A week after my dad's funeral—the first time I'd been back at school since he'd died—I was on the sidewalk after school waiting for my bus and kind of avoiding everybody, when Garf walked up to me and said, "Hey, Stiggy, hey. Sorry to hear about your dad."

"Whatever," I said. I was irritated because I hadn't been thinking about my dad at that exact moment, and Garf had just brought him crashing back into my thoughts.

"It must be really hard," he said.

"Not really." I did not want to talk to this pointy-nosed kid about my dad. I turned away and started walking.

Garf caught up to me and said, "I kind of know what you're going through. My brother killed himself, you know."

"I know that." I started to turn away, then hesitated and asked, "Why?"

Garf shrugged. "Nobody knows. He just did it."

"What, did he OD or something?"

"He shot himself in the face."

I was shocked—not so much because his brother had shot himself but because I couldn't believe that the rumors had been so wrong.

"I don't tell people that. Usually. But, you know, I figured you'd get it."

"Why?" I was genuinely confused. "Because my dad died?"

"No, because he shot himself."

There was a sound that was not a sound, a hollowness, a vacuum, a blankness. Garf's mouth was moving, but I couldn't hear him; I felt this pressure on my ears and the silent thudding of my pulse. My own mouth was moving and I couldn't hear myself either, but I knew what I was saying. *"No, he didn't."*

Garf took a step back and held up his palms. He was still talking and I still couldn't hear anything at all, but I wanted desperately for him to stop. I moved toward him, and his eyes got big. He backed away quickly and was swallowed by the crowd.

My hearing came back, and the first thing I heard was my own breathing. Then the rumble of the bus engines. Then the buzz and chatter and shouts of everybody piling inside. I couldn't stand the thought of being trapped in a bus with all those voices. I forced my fists to unclench and turned away. I walked all the way home staring at my feet and imagining punching Garf Neff right on the tip of his pointy nose.

Mom didn't argue or try to change the subject when I asked her point-blank how Dad had died. She lowered herself onto the sofa and told me to sit down.

"Dad's having a hard time." She spoke in a flat

voice, her usually mobile face hardly moving, her dry eyes darting off to the side as if Dad might be in the next room listening. "I mean, he *was* having a hard time. He'd been fighting this thing for years—since before you were born, actually."

"Fighting what thing?" I asked.

"Well, he wasn't a happy person, you know."

I'd never really thought about that. His happiness.

"And sometimes he'd get very, very sad. He took medicine, and that helped. He took it every day, even though he didn't like the way the medicine made him feel. But sometimes his sadness was more than the pills could handle."

I got it then, what she was saying, but she was talking to me like I was a little kid, and that made me mad.

"You mean he had *depression*," I said.

She jerked back as if I'd slapped her.

"I'm not four years old, Mom. I know about depression."

Mom blinked. Her eyes darted to the next room again. "'Depression' is an ugly word. We never talked to you about it because Dad didn't want you to worry. When things were bad, he worked really, really hard to act like everything was okay. Sometimes even I didn't know he was having his . . . troubles."

"His *troubles*? You mean when he was *depressed*," I said.

She seemed to sink into the sofa, to grow smaller.

"Garf Neff told me Dad shot himself," I said.

She breathed out. I could hear the air hissing from her throat. It went on for a long time before she stopped and breathed in again.

"I didn't want to tell you," she said.

*"Why?"*

She didn't say anything for a few seconds, then, "The last few months were hard for him. Since the accident."

I thought for a second she meant that Dad shooting himself had been an accident. Then I realized she was talking about the *other* accident—the forklift accident that had happened back in October.

# The Other Accident

**Dad blamed it on the forklift. He said the** brakes went out. He'd crashed a two-thousand-pound pallet of car batteries into a shelving structure, causing a couple hundred thousand dollars of damage and almost killing himself and two of the floor workers. Fortunately, nobody was hurt, but Dad was put on leave. He thought he was going to get fired. That was a bad few weeks—all he did was sit around the house talking about how it wasn't his fault.

The investigation didn't really solve anything. The forklift had been wrecked so badly that they couldn't say for sure whether it was because of a mechanical problem or operator error. They finally let him go back to work, but they wouldn't let him run a forklift anymore. They gave him a desk job. He hated that so much, it was like a fog of dark coming off him.

Mom, sunk into the sofa, not looking at me, said, "Your dad loved driving that forklift, even though he complained about it. But that desk was poison to him. Some days he'd leave for work and just go to the park by the river and sit there all day. I didn't know he was doing that until one day his boss called looking for him."

"Was that the day he . . . ?"

"Yes. He drove to East River Park and sat on a bench, and that's where he . . ."

"Shot himself."

She nodded.

"But we don't even have a gun!"

"He bought it the day before. It was one of those guns people use for hunting ducks."

"A shotgun?"

"Yes." Her voice was flat and calm, but her face looked about to shatter.

I wanted to ask *Why*, but what came out of my mouth was, "How?"

She hesitated, her shoulders seemed to slump even more, then she said, "He held it between his legs, and he shot himself in the neck. He might have been trying to shoot himself in the head, but he missed."

I laughed. There was nothing funny—in fact, it was the unfunniest thing ever—but this laugh came ripping out of my throat like vomit, erupting without reason or warning.

Mom collapsed in on herself as if my laugh had crumbled her bones.

I should have felt horrible—I *did* feel horrible—but mostly it made me angry. Angry at both of them. I stood up and walked away, leaving her slumped on the sofa like a broken doll.

Dad had bought the Mustang the summer before he died. It wasn't one of the ones with the big engines. Not the GT. Not the Shelby. Not the Boss. Just a plain old Mustang, used, with a little six-cylinder engine. But it was black with red leather seats, which was cool, and it had a kick-ass sound system with a subwoofer under the backseat.

Mom stored it in the garage after he was gone. She told me it was mine, but I had to wait until I graduated to drive it. If I needed to drive someplace, I had to borrow her Toyota, which was a hassle for both of us.

After Mom told me about how Dad had really died, I went out to the garage and started up the Mustang. I'd been doing that every other day just to keep the battery charged, and to listen to music. I'd synced my phone to the stereo so I could listen to my tunes, hiphop mostly, for the beats and the energy. That day I cranked up some Dre. Old-school. Something about those big beats coming off the subwoofer calmed me.

It was weird sitting in his car. The last time Dad

used it he had driven over to East River Park. The
police had towed it to the impound lot. The only time
I'd driven it was from the impound lot to our garage,
where it had been sitting ever since.

Sometimes I thought I could still smell him—a
faint odor of work sweat, and those licorice candies
he used to suck on to keep himself from smoking cigarettes. Sometimes I had a few seconds when I thought
he was still alive.

A funny thing happened a couple months after my
dad shot himself. Not that it was *funny* funny, unless
you have a sick sense of humor. I was thinking about
forklifts, and wound up on YouTube watching clips
of forklift accidents. Apparently people think forklift accidents are amusing, and they are, I suppose, if
you're not the guy on the forklift. Or his kid. I watched
a bunch. Some of them were pretty sensational.

One of the most spectacular ones showed a forklift
ramming into some big metal shelves, floor to ceiling, all loaded with big crates. The shelves collapse
like dominoes, and the crates come crashing down
into the aisle and hit the row of shelves on the other
side of the warehouse, and they come crashing down
too. The entire warehouse is completely destroyed in
this huge chain reaction. I was watching it for the third
time when I noticed a sign on the wall: WEST CENTRAL
DISTRIBUTING.

My dad worked at West Central Distributing.

I watched it about ten more times. It was one of those grainy surveillance videos and kind of hard to see, but I'm pretty sure it was my dad driving that forklift.

Garf and I had gotten to be friends by that time. After the day he told me about my dad, I ran into him at Brain Food, and we talked about comics, and that was cool. He never said much about his brother, and I didn't talk about my dad, but it was always there. Like, we'd been there. Both of us.

I sent him a link to the forklift video. He texted me back: LOL. Cool.

I got really mad for a few minutes—but then I realized he had no idea it was my dad driving the forklift. He probably didn't even know what my dad did for a living.

I didn't have many friends. In fact, Garf was pretty much it.

The thing with Garf was that I could say anything, and he was fine with it; we were okay. Almost as if he wasn't there, like he was this shadow. No, not a shadow, more like an observer—someone there to remind me that I was real, that I was in the world. Maybe it was the same for him. Anyway, there was this connection.

Later I got connected to Gaia, but that was different.

# The Thing That Happened at Wigglesworth's

**The first time I did anything with Gaia—**
I guess you'd call it a date—I got us kicked out of
Wigglesworth's Juiceteria. I remember what I was
wearing: my usual jeans and one of my dad's flannel
shirts. Gaia had on black jeans and a black T-shirt
with a print on the front: an orange rectangle with a
bright yellow blob in the middle.

We spent a while looking over the chalkboard menu.
All the drinks had weirdly aggressive names—Cherry
Bomb, Brain Freeze, Killer Kiwi—things like that.

I figured Gaia would order a Black Mamba—it
sounded cool—but she went for the Nuclear Sunrise,
a neon-yellow concoction with swirls of mango puree.

I'd never had a Black Mamba, so I ordered one.

As we carried our drinks to a table, I looked at her smoothie and said, "That thing looks like it could fry your retinas."

"It matches my shirt."

"What is that, anyway?"

"A Georgia O'Keeffe painting."

"I've heard of her."

"Yeah, well, she's kind of famous."

I couldn't tell if she was being sarcastic.

The Black Mamba was totally disgusting, like sugary dirt mixed with snail slime. I took a few sips, but it just kept getting worse.

"Try this," I said, pushing the Mamba toward Gaia.

She looked at it suspiciously, sniffed it, lifted out the straw, deposited a single drop of gray slime onto the tip of her pinky, and touched it to her tongue.

"Earthy," she said.

I took another sip, just to remind myself how awful it was.

"If you don't like it, why drink it?" Gaia asked.

"I'm taking it back," I said.

The girl working the counter listened as I told her the Black Mamba she had made for me tasted like crap.

"It's a *Mamba*," she said, as if that explained anything.

"I know what it's called. It's undrinkable."

"Mambas are *supposed* to taste bad," she said.

"Then why do you make them?"

She shrugged. "Some people think if it tastes bad, it must be good for you."

"Well, I don't want it. They should write on the menu that it tastes horrible."

"You want me to dump it for you?"

"I want you to replace it with something drinkable."

"You already drank half of it."

"More like a third. You want that back too?"

She looked askance at my rejected drink. "I'd have to ask my boss."

She didn't move.

"So ask him."

"He's not here," she said.

"Then why don't you give me something that doesn't taste like crap and tell him later."

The girl gave me this pissy look and said, "I think maybe you'd better leave."

"Not till you give me my money back."

She didn't say anything, just pulled her phone out of her pocket and punched in three numbers. A second later she said, "I got this guy here who refuses to leave. . . . Yeah. Yeah, I feel threatened. . . . Wigglesworth's, on Pine Street. . . . Okay." She hung up. "You better go," she said.

That was when I dumped the Black Mamba onto the counter. The girl jumped back to keep from getting splashed, but she didn't quite make it. I went back to the table. Gaia was watching.

"You sure know how to get along with people."

"She was being a bitch."

Gaia hitched her purse up over her shoulder and stood up. We headed for the door and almost made it out of there before the cops showed up. But we didn't quite.

There's not much more to the Wigglesworth's story. I explained to the cops what had happened and tried to get them to try a Black Mamba so they could taste for themselves how bad it was. They wouldn't do it. The counter girl lied and told them I threw the drink at her. I said I'd accidentally tipped it over. Gaia claimed she hadn't seen anything but supported my contention that the Mamba was epically awful. The cops were amused at first, then bored. They told me to leave and not come back, and that was it. Except, after that, if we wanted something fun to drink, we had to go all the way over to the Main Squeeze and drink bubble tea.

Gaia didn't hold the Wigglesworth's thing against me, even though she didn't get a chance to finish her smoothie. She let me gripe about it for a block. I was saying how I was going to put up a bunch of bad reviews online, when she stopped abruptly.

"You know, maybe if you'd been nicer, she would have made you a new drink. She probably made it exactly like she was supposed to. I mean, she just works there."

That took me by surprise; I didn't know what to say. She started walking again. I fell in beside her.

I said, "Maybe. But she should know how crappy her product is. It's my responsibility as a consumer to provide helpful feedback."

Gaia laughed. "Where did you hear *that*?"

"From my dad." I thought about that for a second. "He thought it was important to tell people when they did something wrong."

"Yeah? How did that work out for him?"

I stopped walking. She looked back at me—I think my mouth was hanging open—and she said, "Oh shit. I'm sorry! I'm sorry! That was stupid."

I drew a breath. "It's okay," I said. "Forget about it."

"Sometimes stuff just comes out."

"Yeah, me too."

"I know. I think we're kind of the same. Only I'm more sappy."

"Sappy?"

"Puppies make me cry."

We kept going, neither of us talking. It was okay. I was imagining Gaia holding a puppy and crying. I had no idea why that would make her cry. I was just glad she was walking next to me.

# "Tom Sawyer"

## Rush
## 4:34

**The Mark Twain signs start showing up as** soon as I hit Missouri.

Mark Twain grew up in Hannibal, a little river town on the Mississippi—that's where he set his famous books about Tom Sawyer and Huckleberry Finn. I read *Tom Sawyer* when I was in fourth grade, but I couldn't hack *Huck Finn*, which starts out pretty good but then slows way down.

I used to read a lot, but since Dad died, not so much.

I can tell from the billboards that Hannibal is a tourist trap. The ads are for things like the Becky Thatcher House and the Huck Finn Freedom Center. There is the Mark Twain Brewing Company, the Mark Twain Dinette, Mark Twain's boyhood home, a Mark

Twain Cave tour. . . . I remember the part where Tom Sawyer and Becky Thatcher get lost in a cave, and they think Injun Joe wants to kill them, and Tom finds a fortune in gold coins. I quit reading the billboards and think about caves. I don't want to think about caves. Caves make me think about Gaia.

I speed up, thinking that if I drive fast enough to scare myself, I'll be able to quit thinking about Gaia. The road is a bumpy little two-lane highway. I've got the Mustang up to about eighty, when a bird hits the windshield. I think it's a blue jay. I slow down. Coming around a curve, I see a figure up ahead, standing on the shoulder with his thumb out.

I pull over because I feel bad about the blue jay, and because I think the guy must have been standing there for days, and because I really need to talk to somebody who is not already living inside my head.

# Wonder Woman

**Every time I saw Gaia, I learned something** about her that surprised me. For example, I met her at Starbucks one day in June. I was late. She had her earbuds in and was watching a movie on her phone.

"*Dirty Dancing*," she said. She told me she'd watched it ten times. "Sometimes I finish and go right back to the beginning and watch it over again." She pocketed her phone. "I told you I was sappy. And if you ever tell anybody, I'll kill you."

"I watched it once," I said. "But I didn't make it to the end."

"The end is the best part, but you probably wouldn't like it."

"I bet you liked *Titanic*."

"Hated it."

"Me too. *Wonder Woman?*"

Gaia smiled, and it was like a light came on inside her face.

"Me too," I said.

The next day she came over to my house to see my Wonder Woman doll. Yes, I had a Wonder Woman doll. It used to be my mom's, from the 1970s, still in its original box, with a gray Diana Prince uniform you could put on her.

Wonder Woman was on my Darth Vader shelf. I wasn't really into Star Wars anymore, but when I was a kid, I was obsessed with Darth, my main man. I had a whole shelf full of Vader toys, from the little tiny figurines to a red lightsaber to a helmet that used to fit on my head. It had a sort of membrane on the mouth to make your voice sound funny.

Gaia didn't care about Darth Vader, but she was impressed by Wonder Woman.

"You never took her out of the box?"

"My mom says it's worth more money this way."

"Kind of a waste."

"I was more into Vader."

"Wonder Woman would kick his ass." She looked over my collection. "You must have every Darth Vader toy ever."

"Not even close. There are thousands."

She put Wonder Woman back onto the shelf.

"I know, it's stupid," I said. "I was a kid."

"I bet you could sell all this stuff to that comic book shop," she said.

She turned to my bookcase and checked out the titles. The Star Wars novels were on the middle shelf, but the rest of the books—stacked every which way and piled high on top—were mostly horror and vampire stories. I even had my copy of *Bunnicula* from the third grade. It's about a rabbit with fangs. Naturally, that was the one she pulled out and started paging through.

"I read this," she said.

I reached past her and grabbed my copy of *It*, by Stephen King, the fattest book I owned. "You should read this one."

Gaia wrinkled her nose. "I don't like scary books. I only like fake-scary books." She looked around at the rest of my junk. "Your room is really messy."

"I know where everything is."

She knelt down and started moving my books around, straightening them up and arranging them. She was so intense about it that I just stood back and watched.

"Um . . . do you want a soda or something?" I asked after a minute.

"Do you have any fizzy water?"

"I think so." I left her with the books and went to the kitchen. There was no fizzy water in the fridge, but I knew we had a whole case of the stuff. Ever since Dad died, Mom had been going crazy at Sam's Club, buying massive quantities of everything—cases of canned goods, laundry detergent, water, huge bundles of paper towels and toilet paper. Cartons were stacked on and in front of Dad's workbench in the garage and on either side of his car. We were ready for the zombie invasion.

It took me a couple minutes of moving boxes around to find the bottled water. It was hiding under a lifetime supply of facial tissues.

The water was warm, of course, so I had to put it in glasses with ice. By the time I got back to my room with the water, Gaia had finished organizing my books and was making my bed. She had also picked up all my dirty clothes from the floor and piled them in the laundry basket.

It was embarrassing, to say the least.

"I didn't know you were such a neat freak," I said.

"I didn't know you were so gross."

There was a moment when I thought maybe we were going to have an argument, but then, like flipping a switch, we were both laughing.

"God, we are such weirdos," she said.

I handed her a glass of water; she took it, and our fingers touched. It felt electric. Not like a static electricity shock, but more like a low, buzzy current that lasted for a few seconds even after our hands separated.

It was the first time we had physically touched.

Okay, that's weird. Because we'd been seeing each other on and off for a couple of weeks. It wasn't that I didn't *want* to touch her. Some days I thought about nothing else. But she had this invisible shell, and I was afraid that if I reached out to hold her hand, she'd recoil, and I couldn't stand the thought of that.

Now we had touched fingers, and we were still okay. She acted as if nothing had happened. But it had.

If we had been in a movie like *Dirty Dancing*, we would have crashed into each other's embrace and kissed until our oxygen ran out. But it wasn't like that at all. It was more like we were two cats touching noses, then backing off.

I was telling Garf about Gaia hanging out in my bedroom and organizing my books and making my bed. A lot of guys would have asked me if we'd made out, but not Garf. Instead he asked me how she had arranged my books.

"With her hands?" I said.

"No, I mean was it alphabetical by author, or by size, or by the color of the spine?"

"Why would anybody organize books by color?" I asked.

"I saw it in a magazine. It's kind of cool-looking."

"I think by author."

"That's cool." Everything was always cool with Garf. "So are you guys, like, into each other?"

"I don't know. It's like we're doing this thing where we try to find things we both like, you know? Only, she doesn't like horror stories and I don't like *Dirty Dancing*."

"What's that?"

"This old romance movie. There are a lot of things we both hate, but we both like Wonder Woman."

"I liked the movie. Hey, I know what you could do. The Fourth is coming up. Maybe she likes fireworks."

I should've known better than to listen to Garf.

"Fireworks are lame," Gaia said.

"Lame?"

"Fireworks are a glorification of masculine aggression. Like 'The Star-Spangled Banner.'"

"Oh," I said. "Like Wonder Woman?"

"*Not* like Wonder Woman. You know what we should do? We should go to the quietest place we can find—someplace with no fireworks."

I was stunned by that—by the fact that she assumed we would be spending the Fourth of July together.

"Like a library?" I said.

"They won't be open on the Fourth. You know what we should do? We should go to the mushroom caves."

The *caves*. The caves were legendary. I had never been there, but I'd been hearing about them for years.

"Okay," I said.

"Nobody'll be there," she said. "They'll all be out gawking at the explosions."

"Okay," I said. "Have you ever been?"

"I don't even know where they are, but they're supposed to be cool."

# Grant

**The mushroom caves, I learned online, were** not natural caves. They were a network of silica mine shafts dug into the cliffs back in the nineteenth century. "Silica" is another name for "sand." Why people needed to mine sand, I don't know. It doesn't seem like it would be that hard to find. Maybe there was a sand shortage. Later, the shafts were called the mushroom caves because back in the 1930s, after the sand mining stopped, the caves were converted into an underground mushroom farm. That didn't last long. A few years later the caves were closed off and nobody used them.

I got all that off the internet. What I didn't find on the internet was how to get there. For that I had to go to the outernet, which meant texting and talking with real-life people who had been to the caves. Like Grant McMann.

Grant was my cousin on my mom's side. He was the same age as me, and we went to the same school, but we couldn't have been more different. Grant was a football player who looked like a two-hundred-pound advertisement for whole milk, beef, and white bread. Also, he was a total dick—the kind of guy who would come up behind you in school and dope slap you so hard, you'd go skidding down the hall on your belly.

In other words, he was the kind of guy I tried to avoid.

But I knew Grant had been to the mushroom caves, so I sent him a text. About thirty seconds later my phone rang. Grant.

"Hi," I said.

"Twiggy!" he bellowed. Twiggy was his name for me. I hated it.

"Yeah," I said. "So, you been to the caves lately?"

"Oh, hell yeah! We hauled a keg in last weekend. It was off the hook, dude. You going?"

"Thinking about it." The idea of being underground in the dark with a bunch of beer-drinking jocks was not an attractive proposition. "I was hoping you could tell me how to get there."

"You never been, Twig? Don't forget to bring candles!" He laughed. I had no idea what was so funny.

"So how do I find it?"

"Well, they put up a new gate, so you can't just walk in like we used to. But I can show you."

I did not want to go to the caves with Grant. I did not want to go *anywhere* with Grant.

"When did you want to go?" he asked.

"I was thinking Friday."

"No can do. Friday's the Fourth, dude. I'm headed up to the lake to blow shit up. Adrian just got back from South Dakota with a whole trunk full of fireworks. It's gonna be epic. You want to come?"

"No, thanks. I'm supposed to meet somebody at the caves. Maybe you can just tell me how to get there."

"Okay, sure. It's kind of complicated. . . ."

# "Dem Bones"

## ("The Skeleton Dance")
## 1:57

**I roll down the passenger window. The hitch-**hiker doesn't look any better up close, but no worse, either. He frowns at the scratch on the passenger door.

"Looks like you got keyed, man," he says.

"Yeah, I got keyed. Where you headed?"

"Hannibal," he says. Hannibal is forty miles down-river.

"Hop in," I say.

He shrugs off his backpack, tosses it in back, and climbs in front, bringing with him the smell of diesel exhaust, road dust, and body odor.

"Name's Bob," he says. "But you can call me 'Knob.' Everybody else does." He's older than I thought at first—maybe in his forties. He grins, and I see he's missing one canine tooth.

I check my mirror and pull back onto the highway.

"I'm Stiggy," I say.

"Cool," he says. "You going to Hannibal too?"

"I'm just driving," I say.

"Cool." We ride along without talking for a few minutes. I swerve around a dead opossum. Back in Iowa most of the roadkill was raccoons, but now in Missouri all I see is squashed possums with their naked tails.

"I come down from Rhinelander," Knob says.

"Where's that?"

"Wisconsin."

We pass another billboard advertising Mark Twain's childhood home.

"Mark Twain," Knob says. "I read a book he wrote."

"Which one?" I ask.

"The one about the dog. Something about the wild."

"*The Call of the Wild*? That's Jack London."

Bob frowns. "Pretty sure it was Mark Twain."

I decide not to argue.

A minute later he says. "Maybe it *was* Jack London."

"Mark Twain wrote *Huckleberry Finn*."

"Oh. Yeah. You got that right. My bad."

"What's in Hannibal?" I ask.

"Mark Twain." He laughs and slaps his thigh, raising a puff of dust. A second later he says, "I got a job waiting on me. At least I think I do. Farmwork. You ever do farmwork?"

"Nope."

"It ain't the easiest way to make a living, I'll tell you that."

"I suppose somebody's got to do it."

"You got that right." He takes a hand-rolled cigarette out of his shirt pocket. "Mind if I fire one up?"

"Crack the window," I say.

He opens his window a couple of inches, then struggles with a disposable lighter, clicking it about ten times before he gets a flame. He inhales, holds it, and lets it out. It's not tobacco.

He offers me a hit.

"No, thanks," I say. Weed just makes me sad.

"Suit yourself." He takes another drag. I crack my window too. He takes a couple more hits, then spits onto his palm, douses the joint, and slips it back into his shirt pocket.

"How'd you get that name, Stiggy?" he asks.

"It's from my initials, SG."

"Cool."

I don't ask him why he's called Knob, but he tells me anyway.

"I got stuck with 'Knob' twenty years ago on account of military school. First year, they called all us noobs 'Knob.' Like we were a thing. Didn't last, though." He laughs. "Five weeks. They kicked me out. But the name stuck on me."

"I quit school," I say.

"How come?"

"Too many assholes."

"I feel ya, man. Being human's a bitch. Some days I wish I was a dog."

Again we lapse into silence. Knob's chin drops to his chest. I think he might be asleep. A couple of minutes later he rouses himself and looks at me. I hadn't noticed before, but his eyes are two different colors—one blue, one green.

"Listen," he says. "Seriously. Do you know who you are?"

"I know who I am." Saying it out loud makes me wonder if it's true.

"You sure? Suppose you take off that cap. You still you without John Deere on your noggin?"

"Sure."

"Because you think it's obvious? Suppose you get a haircut. Still you?"

Sounds like a trick question, so I just shrug.

"Suppose you chop off your little finger. Still you?"

"What's your point?"

"Suppose I could take out your brain and hook you up to some tubes and wires so you could still think. You ever see that movie?"

"I think I saw that on *Doctor Who*. Or maybe it was *Star Trek*."

"Yeah. Would you still be you?"

"I hope I never find out."

"What about if you get killed. You think you have, like, a soul or something?"

"I haven't decided."

"Well, it don't matter, but it proves you don't really know who you are. But I do."

"Okay," I said. "Who am I?"

"You're a point, man. A location. A nexus."

"Great. I always wanted to be a nexus."

"We all are, man." He takes the joint out of his pocket, digs out his lighter, flicks it a few times, curses, flicks it some more. No luck. He tosses the lighter out the window. "Got a light, dude?"

"Sorry."

"These new cars suck, man."

"Ten years old isn't exactly new," I point out.

"It's all relative, man. Use to be, every car had a lighter. Now they don't even have ashtrays. Screw it." He tucks the dead joint back into his pocket. "Later, man," he says. I'm not sure if he's talking to me, himself, or the joint. We ride in silence for a few minutes.

"So, what's a nexus?" I ask.

"A connection, man. That's it. It's what we are. Like, most people think they're a soul stuck inside a sack of skin full of muscle and blood. They think all the stuff around them—their clothes, this car, the air, the trees, the people—they think that's something else, but the thing is, who we are is the sum of all the things we're connected to. Like, your knee bone connected to your thigh bone, your thigh bone connected to your hip bone. You know that song?"

"I think I heard it once."

"It's called 'Dem Bones.' My gramps used to sing it. Anyways, who you are is a nexus, a clot of electrical impulses inside a meat puppet wrapped in cotton and leather and polyester inside this piece-a-crap lighterless vehicle on this strip of asphalt. You're just a particular point that happens to be in the middle of it. It gets bigger—or infinite, depending how you look at it. You are your family, you're your friends, you're me, and I'm you. You're everybody you know and everybody you've ever met, and if you want to get, like, cosmic, you're also the people you haven't met yet, the places you're gonna go, the things you're gonna do. That's who you are. You know John Donne?"

"Nope."

"Well, he's been dead a few hundred years, so I ain't surprised. He wrote this poem, 'No Man Is an Island.' You know it?"

"It sounds familiar."

"You should look it up. Dude knew some shit."

# The Caves

**"Are we lost?" Gaia asked.**

"I don't know."

"If you don't know if we're lost, then we're lost."

We were in my dad's Mustang. It was a risk, taking it without permission. Mom had left me on my own while she attended a two-day yoga retreat up in Bayfield, where they sit in these really hot rooms and sweat out all their problems. I wanted to show Gaia my future ride, so I took the Mustang. As long as I didn't wreck it, Mom would never know.

It was a sunny and hot Fourth of July. We had the air-conditioning cranked. Even if we never found the caves, I told myself, it was a nice day for a drive in the country. We were up on the bluffs, looking for a nameless dirt road that led down a coulee to the cave entrance. Grant had told me there was no sign, but he'd said, *You can't miss it.*

"Grant said to turn onto Pike Road, then right on the first road after the goat farm. Did you see a goat farm?"

"How does a goat farm look any different from any other farm?"

"They have goats, I guess."

"Is that a goat?"

I slowed down. "I think that's a sheep." A few seconds later I spotted a small sign ahead: GRISWOLD'S GOATS.

"Ha!" I said. "Told you."

Off to the left was a large grassy field, and yes, there were goats grazing. A few hundred yards later we came to a dirt road leading off to the right. I hit the brakes, too late to make the turn. Gaia lurched forward but was saved by her shoulder belt. "This must be it." I put the car in reverse and backed up.

Gaia was leaning forward, reaching for something on the floor.

"Did you lose this?" she asked. "It must have been under the seat."

I stopped the car. "Let me see." It was an iPod. My dad's, I supposed, although I hadn't known he had one. "It must be ancient—it doesn't even have a camera." I tried to turn it on, but the screen stayed black. "Battery must be dead." I stuck it into the glove compartment and turned onto the unmarked road.

"Are you sure this is a road? It looks more like somebody's driveway."

"We'll find out." The road angled down, twisting and turning. It was so narrow, I worried about cars coming from the other direction, but none did. We went over a wooden bridge and continued to descend. "It's too long to be a driveway," I said.

The road narrowed even more; plants were dragging against the sides of the car. After about half a mile the trees thinned and we could see the river. The road jogged hard right. We kept going, the bluffs rising on one side, a swampy morass on the other. Soon we arrived at a sort of gravel pit cut into the side of the bluff. There was one other car there—a Chevy Tahoe. I pulled in next to it.

"I guess we won't be the only ones in there," Gaia said.

At the far side of the sand pit was an opening about ten feet high in the sandstone bluff. The opening was blocked by a set of rusty steel bars.

I turned off the car.

"How do we get in?" Gaia asked.

"Grant said there's an opening." I grabbed my backpack from the backseat and got out. As we approached the opening, I could see that the bars were part of a locked gate set into a steel frame solidly embedded in the sandstone. The gate had been welded shut. Gaia pointed out a well-worn path leading off to the right.

The path zigzagged up through a tumble of boulders

and into some stunted trees growing sideways out of the bluff. The path hooked back around and ended up on a ledge about four feet above the steel gate. An opening had been hacked into the soft limestone behind the top of the steel frame. Probably Grant or one of his buddies swinging a pickax. There was just enough room to squeeze down between the bars and the rock and climb down the inside of the gate.

"I guess this is how we get in," I said. "You sure you want to?"

"You brought a flashlight, right?"

"Two flashlights."

"What if we get lost?"

"I brought water and granola bars too." I examined the opening, then took off my backpack and handed it to Gaia. "I'll go first, and you hand this down to me."

"Okay."

I slid over the edge of the ledge, grasped the top of the steel frame, and eased my legs into the opening. As I lowered myself behind the gate, it occurred to me that getting out again would not be easy. We'd have to climb up the gate and pull ourselves up through the opening. I was pretty sure we could do it—I mean, everybody else who had been in the caves had gotten out. At least I hoped so.

A few seconds later I was standing at the bottom, looking out through the bars.

"Okay," I said. I saw Gaia's face above me, then my backpack.

"Can you catch it?" she called down.

"I think so."

She dropped the backpack; I caught it and set it aside.

"Here I come," she said, and I was looking at the bottoms of her sneakers.

I reached up and grabbed her ankles. "I got you."

"Don't let go," she said.

She lowered herself slowly, climbing hand over hand down the gate until we were standing side by side, our backs to the gate, looking into the darkness.

"Now what?" she said.

# Chiropterans

**We shined our flashlights into an arched** passageway about fifteen feet high. The floor was sandy and flat, with thousands of footprints and lots of garbage: beer cans; food wrappers; discarded clothing; a rusted, twisted bicycle frame with no wheels.

"Why would anyone bring a bike in here?" I wondered aloud.

"People are weird," Gaia said.

We couldn't see the end of the tunnel—it went straight into the bluff for as far as our flashlights could penetrate. We walked forward, neither of us speaking, following a snaking path through the scattered trash. The caves smelled like wet sand with a slight sour tang. After about two minutes of walking, we came to a wall with passages heading off to the left and the right. I could see from the footprints and trail of trash that most people turned left. The passage to the right sloped up slightly.

"Maybe we should leave a trail of bread crumbs," Gaia said.

"Oops. Forgot the bread."

"We'll just have to keep track, then. How big do you think this place is?"

"Grant said he got lost for, like, an hour once. But he was drunk."

"If we make only right turns, then to get back, all we have to do is make only left turns."

I had a feeling that didn't make sense, but I couldn't find the flaw in her logic.

"You want to turn right, then?"

"Might as well."

We set off up the less-used, right-hand passage. There wasn't as much trash on the floor, but I noticed as we moved deeper into the passageway that the sand underfoot was getting darker, and the sour smell became stronger, and I heard a faint rustling sound.

"What's that noise?" Gaia asked.

We stopped, and I shined my light around the tunnel. There was something odd about the ceiling.

"Oh my God," Gaia whispered. "Are those *bats*?"

Those were bats, thousands of them, covering the ceiling above us.

It took us about ten seconds to run all the way back to the intersection. We stopped there, gasping for breath.

Gaia was gagging and coughing.

"It's okay," I said.

"Okay?" She made a retching sound. "I feel like my lungs are coated with bat poop."

I reached back and pulled a water bottle from my backpack. "Here."

She drank, and then I drank.

"Can you get rabies from bat poop?" she asked.

"I don't think so." I hoped not. "Do you want to leave?"

"Just give me a second."

We drank more water.

"Grant said there might be some bats."

"Thanks for the heads-up." She was bent forward, hands on her knees. I thought she might be about to throw up.

"You want to go?" I asked.

She stood up straight and shook her head. "As long as we're here, we should look around."

"So . . . left turn?"

"Left turn."


The tunnel with all the footprints and garbage had no bats. I kept shining my light up to check. We had gone about a hundred yards when I saw a faint light up ahead. The tunnel curved, then opened up into a circular chamber about half the size of a gymnasium. The back wall was stepped—four big curved tiers, each about three feet high, like a giant stairway to nowhere. There were dozens of candles on the lowest level. Only a few of them were lit. I shined my flashlight around. There were three other openings leading to more passageways. We were alone.

"I wonder who lit the candles," Gaia said.

I shined my light into each of the other openings.

"This looks like a place where they sacrifice virgins," I said.

Gaia gave me a sharp look.

"I didn't mean anything by that," I said.

Her look got sharper. "What makes you think I think you meant something?"

"I don't . . . I mean—"

Just then something came flying out of one of the passageways. For a fraction of a second I thought, *Bat!*

The thing hit the ground. *It's too big to be a bat*, I thought—and then the world exploded.

Intensely bright flashes shot into my eyes, and my eardrums were pummeled by a storm of loud, sharp cracks. I heard a scream. Maybe it was me.

It took me only a second to realize that someone had thrown a large string of firecrackers—not just a string, but a big coil. The chamber was filling with smoke. I clapped my hands over my ears and looked around for Gaia, but I couldn't see her.

"Gaia!" I shouted. I could barely hear my own voice.

The fireworks showed no sign of slowing down—it must have been one of those thousand-firecracker spools. I was looking around frantically, but the flashes from the explosions had left me half-blinded. She must have fled into one of the passages. I picked the closest one and ran into it—and into somebody.

Somebody big. I bounced off and landed on my butt. My flashlight went flying, and broke when it hit the wall. I'd gone about thirty feet into the tunnel, and it was dark. All I could see were afterimages. My ears were ringing, but they weren't ringing so bad that I couldn't hear the laughter. It sounded like at least three guys.

"Oh man, that was epic!" somebody said.

A bright light hit me in the eyes. I put my hand up to block it and tried to see who was holding the flashlight.

"You okay, Twiggy?" I knew that voice. Grant McMann.

I jumped to my feet and ran at him. I didn't care what happened to me, I just wanted to smash my fists into his face.

"Whoa!" he said, grabbing my wrists in an iron grip. "Down, boy!"

"You *asshole!*" I screamed and struggled in his grip, and tried to kick him in the nuts, but he saw it coming and blocked my foot with his massive thigh. It was like kicking a rock.

"Easy, Twig. It was just a joke."

"Joke? Where's Gaia? Did she come this way?"

"She took off, dude," one of the other guys said. There were four of them: Grant; his best friend, Adrian Youngblood; Ben Gingrass, the enormous nose tackle for the football team; and Vern Sommers, who'd gotten kicked off the team for drinking.

"Where?" I shouted.

"Back the way you came in. You should've seen her face when those things started going off!"

I turned and headed back toward the chamber.

"Twig! Wait up!"

I ignored him. The firecrackers were still going off, lighting up the end of the tunnel. When I got there, the chamber was so full of smoke, I could hardly see across it. I started coughing. I shielded my eyes and ran past the exploding string and into the other passageway, still coughing. I'd gotten only a few steps in when I realized that I had no light.

"Gaia!" I yelled, then listened. All I heard were explosions. I took a deep breath, held it, and ran back into the smoke-filled chamber. I grabbed two lit candles and made my way back to the passageway where Adrian said she had gone, one flickering candle in each hand. Behind me the firecrackers were slowing down. Ahead was only darkness.

# Bottle Rockets

**The candles were barely enough to light the** ground three feet in front of me. I couldn't see the ceiling, or even the walls unless I got close to them. It was like walking through an infinite black space, with garbage underfoot.

I had to walk slowly to keep the candles burning. By the time I reached the steel gate, the candles were burned halfway down. Gaia wasn't there. I looked up at the gap between the limestone and the gate frame. Could she have climbed out? Would she do that? Would she leave me there?

I didn't think so. She had to be in the caves. I hoped she still had her flashlight. I headed back in. It took only a few minutes to reach the chamber. The firecrackers were done. A chest-high layer of smoke hung in the air. I waded into the stinky cloud and shouted, "Gaia!"

I listened and heard something that might have been laughter, then nothing.

My candles were almost burned out, so I lit a couple of fresh ones from the ones on the giant steps and stuck a couple more into my pockets.

*Now which way?* I wondered. There were four choices: the way I'd come in, two unknowns, and the one where I'd run into Grant and his friends. After a moment of indecision, I went for the tunnel where I'd met Grant. I hated to admit it, but I needed his help. Grant knew his way around the caves, and those guys would have flashlights.

It didn't take long to find them. Almost as soon as I was in the tunnel, I heard a sharp explosion, then guys laughing. I followed the sound into a side passageway, and saw a light ahead.

Grant and Adrian and the other two guys were sitting against the four walls of a chamber about twenty feet across. In the middle of the room, four flashlights were balanced on their bases, shining straight up. As I entered, there was a fizzing sound and a blinding streak of light followed by a loud bang. All four of them shrieked with laughter. It took me a second to get what had happened, and I couldn't believe it. Grant had fired a bottle rocket at Adrian, who was sitting against the opposite wall.

"Damn, that was close," Adrian said. "My turn!"

He fumbled with a lighter and lit the fuse of his own bottle rocket. The rocket leaped from his fingers and corkscrewed across the chamber. Grant dove to the side, and the rocket exploded against the wall where his head had been. More laughter, from all four of them.

"Hey," I said.

They all looked at me.

"New player!" Adrian shrieked.

"No, thanks," I said. "Have you guys seen Gaia?"

"You couldn't find her?" Grant asked.

"Obviously not."

"Maybe she ditched you," said Vern.

"Or maybe you guys scared her so bad that she panicked and got herself lost and she'll never find her way out of here."

They thought that was pretty funny. I forced myself to remain calm. If I lost it, they would just find it even more amusing.

"Look, can I borrow one of your flashlights? I really have to find her."

Ben Gingrass lit another bottle rocket. It shot across the chamber straight at me. I threw up my hands, dropping my candles. The rocket glanced off my elbow and exploded a nanosecond later.

"Shit!" I yelled, it being the only word I could think of.

They thought that was hilarious.

I ran over to their collection of flashlights and, before I could think too much about it, scooped them all up and took off back down the tunnel, followed by a clamor of shouted curses.

I hit the big chamber at a dead run, clutching three flashlights in one arm and holding one in my hand. I picked a passageway at random and ran into it. As soon as I got far enough away, I stopped and turned off all but one of the flashlights. I stuck the extras in my belt, then looked around at the passageway I had entered.

It was much like the other tunnels, with a flat floor and an arched ceiling. I wanted to yell for Gaia, but I was afraid Grant and company would hear me. They might not have flashlights, but they had candles, and they knew these caves a lot better than I did. I continued down the passageway. There were lots of footprints. If Gaia's were among them, I had no way of knowing. I kept walking, silently reaching out with my mind: *Gaia! Gaia! Gaia!*

I thought I'd found her at one point, crumpled, naked, and thrown up against the wall like a broken mannequin. My heart stopped and I was hit by a wave of horrified vertigo—then I saw that it wasn't Gaia. It was exactly what it looked like: a busted-up store mannequin.

I had to take a minute to calm down after that. *She's okay,* I told myself. *I'll find her.*

I edged around the mannequin. It had no hands. That creeped me out worse than anything.

I kept going. After a while the passageways all looked the same—maybe I was going in circles. The first flashlight dimmed and finally quit working altogether. I threw it away and pulled out the next one. Because I didn't know what else to do, I just kept walking, and walking, and thinking about Gaia.

I'd been thinking about Gaia a lot the past few weeks. I'd been thinking about her constantly. She didn't know that. Every time our relationship came up in conversation, she either changed the subject or made it about how I was doing something wrong.

"I like spending time with you," she said once when we were drinking bubble tea at the Squeeze. "When you're not being a dick."

"When am I being a dick?" I asked.

"You told Maeve she was an elitist agri-poser."

Maeve Samms was Gaia's friend. She had a boyfriend who went to school at Macalester, and that bugged me. I mean, I wasn't interested in Maeve, but a college guy going out with a girl in high school felt like poaching.

The week before, we had run into Maeve at a concert at Lake Harriet—some aging punk band from the eighties having a reunion, and it was free. Maeve was going on and on about how her supercool uncle had this supercool organic farm in Wisconsin. That bugged me too—her talking about the farm like it was the Garden of Eden. I thought "elitist agri-poser" was pretty clever, but Maeve had taken it the wrong way. I'd thought she was going to start crying.

"I wasn't trying to be mean," I said to Gaia. "I was just joking around."

"Yeah, well, joking around and acting like an asshole aren't necessarily mutually exclusive. You know Michael has disappeared."

"Who's Michael?"

"Her *boyfriend*? Hannah McCourt's *brother*? Do you even listen?"

"Oh. The college guy."

Gaia rolled her eyes. "Yes, the college guy."

"I didn't know he was Hannah's brother."

"Well, he is. He just took off a few weeks ago. Left school. Nobody knows where he is. Maeve's really upset, and Hannah's freaking."

"Why are we all of a sudden talking about Hannah?"

"God, you are impossible!"

Why was I thinking about that? I came to another intersection. Had I been there before? I looked around, trying to find some familiar piece of trash. Just some beer cans, and there were beer cans everywhere.

I shouted Gaia's name and listened.

I thought I heard something. My name?

"Gaia!" I yelled, so loud it hurt my throat. I listened again.

Nothing, just the faint hiss of air creeping over sandstone, and the almost inaudible murmur of blood coursing through my veins.

I stacked some beer cans in the middle of the passage, so I'd know if I ended up there again, then took the right-hand passage.

Sometimes I wondered if Gaia even liked me. She always seemed to be up for going out and doing something, but it was always me who called her. We'd been to a couple of movies, we'd gone to a beach on the Saint Croix, we'd been to that concert at Powderhorn. In public I tried to match her sullen what*ever*-ness. I thought if I acted like her, it would be more like we were together. As far as I knew, she wasn't seeing anyone else. Did that make her my girlfriend?

Garf thought she was my girlfriend. That's what he called her.

"How's your *girlfriend*?" he would ask. I think he might've been a little jealous, since I hadn't been hanging out with him as much.

"She's not exactly my girlfriend," I told him.

"I don't think she likes me," Garf said.

"I don't think she likes anybody."

Except I hoped she liked me.

I came to another intersection, one I was sure I'd never been to before because one of the passageways was choked with rubble. The tunnel had collapsed. There was only one way to go, so I went that way.

I'd heard Grant and his posse only twice since I'd run off with their flashlights. Just echoey voices in the distance. For the past half hour or so I'd heard only my own footsteps, my own breathing. Still, every time I turned a corner, I expected to run into them. Part of me wished I would—they'd probably kick my ass, but at least I wouldn't be so alone.

I kept going and soon noticed the smell of fireworks. I figured I must be getting close to the candlelit chamber. I stopped and turned off the flashlight. There was a faint glow ahead, and the sound of voices.

A single male voice: "Come on, don't be like that."

Then a louder, girl's voice: "Stop it!"

*Gaia.*

# "Amazing"

## Johnette Napolitano
## 4:08

**Maybe I'm a little high from the second-**hand smoke, or maybe I'm just tired after hours of driving, but after I drop Bob the Knob off at a farm five miles north of Hannibal, my mind is spinning in circles, thinking about what he said, about nexuses, and John Donne, and "Dem Bones." I know I've heard that song, but I can't imagine where. It's not on Dad's iPod.

I'm still thinking about it when I pull into downtown Hannibal, and guess what?

Hannibal sucks.

Just like I knew it would. Mark Twain and Tom Sawyer and Huck Finn everything, right down to the fence that Tom Sawyer supposedly was in charge of painting, even though Tom Sawyer is fictional and so was Mark Twain in a way, because Mark Twain's real name was Samuel Clemens.

I suppose you can't blame Hannibal for turning into a tourist trap. A lot of the small towns along the river are half-abandoned, with nothing left but a dilapidated trailer park, a bar, and a gas station if they're lucky. Hannibal still has a lot of people and businesses, all thanks to their connection with a guy who's been dead a hundred years and who wrote a few books set in a fictionalized version of their town.

I spend an hour walking around gawking at all the phony junk with the rest of the tourists. I stop at a kiosk and take a brochure advertising the Mark Twain Cave tour and sit on a nearby bench and read it. Apparently the cave Samuel Clemens wrote about in *Tom Sawyer* was real. Back in the 1850s some crazy doctor used it for storing dead bodies, and Jesse James once used it as a hideout.

It's twenty bucks for the tour. No caving for me, thanks—not at any price.

Thinking about caves makes me think about Gaia, and thinking about Gaia is not what I want to do right now. The whole reason for this stupid trip is so I can think about other things—or better yet, not think at all.

# Keyed

**I clicked the flashlight back on and ran** toward the light, toward the voices. I heard Gaia yell, "Let me go!" Laughter. I burst into the candlelit chamber. The guy's back was to me; I could see Gaia's face past his shoulder. He was gripping her wrists. I ran straight at them and drove my shoulder into the small of his back. It should have knocked him down, but it didn't. He was too big. He'd played too much football. He just grunted and whirled around and punched me in the chest so hard, I thought my heart stopped.

It was Ben Gingrass. He was still holding on to Gaia with his other hand.

I was gasping for breath, still on my feet but just

barely. Gaia twisted and kicked at his legs and tried to pull free. He looked at her and said, "You're ugly anyway."

He let go. Gaia fell onto her butt. He turned back toward me, his fists bunched, his little eyes glittering in the candlelight.

"The flashlight thief," he said through a teeth-gritting smile. "This should be fun."

I did not think whatever was about to happen would be fun. He brought his right fist back and stepped toward me. I lifted my hands to try to block him, but before he could deliver a punch that would probably break my jaw, Gaia screamed and leaped onto his back.

Ben reached over his shoulder with his left hand, grabbed her by the hair, and threw her off—a casual motion, like taking off a T-shirt. His little eyes never left my face. I was sure I was going to die.

"Hey!" A new voice. It was Grant, holding a candle, standing at the mouth of one of the tunnels.

Ben lowered his fist. Vern and Adrian followed Grant into the chamber.

"What's going on?" Grant asked.

"I caught the flashlight stealer," Ben said.

I thought, *Uh-oh*. I was going to get the crap beat out of me by all four of them.

Grant looked at Gaia, who was on the ground holding her head.

"Are you okay?" Grant asked.

Gaia shook her head.

Grant frowned and said, "We beating up girls now?"

"She jumped me from behind," Ben said.

"He tried to *rape* me," Gaia said.

Ben laughed. It sounded fake. "You're not pretty enough to rape."

"So you only rape *pretty* girls?" Gaia said.

"Ha-ha-ha," Ben said. He looked at Grant. "Nothing happened. Look, she's still got her pants on."

"Lucky for you," Grant said. He turned to me. "How about you, Twig?"

"I'm all right." I was starting to think I might not get killed after all.

"He try to rape you too?" Grant asked.

"Ha-ha-ha," Ben said. "Very funny."

Vern and Adrian were looking on, waiting for a clue as to what to do next. I had the feeling that they could go either way.

Grant pointed with his candle at the two flashlights still stuck in my belt. "Mind giving us our flashlights back?"

I gave him the two flashlights. He handed one to Vern. The one I'd been using a minute before was over by the wall, glowing weakly. Adrian picked it up.

"Where's the other one?" Grant asked.

I shrugged.

"Whatever," he said. "I'm tired. Let's go." He started toward the passage leading to the exit. Vern and Adrian followed. Ben hesitated, then trailed after them, leaving Gaia and me alone. I went over to her and helped her stand up.

"Are you hurt?"

She shook her head, then hugged me.

"What about you?" she said in my ear. "He hit you really hard."

"I don't think anything broke. I was looking for you."

"I got lost. My flashlight died. I thought I'd never find you."

"I was calling."

"I thought I heard you once. Did you hear me?"

"I think so." I held her at arm's length, looked into her candle-sparked eyes.

"We should go," she said.

"Let's wait a minute, give them time to get out. I don't want to run into them again." Mostly I didn't want to let go. I wanted to kiss her so bad, it hurt. But after what had just happened, I was afraid of how she would react. I felt lucky to be touching her at all.

"He said you stole their flashlights."

"Yeah, I did." I was kind of proud of that.

"Like it was my fault what you did. He said I owed him."

"I'm sorry." I wasn't so proud anymore.

"It wasn't your fault. And nothing happened, not really. You came. You saved me."

"I think Grant saved us both."

"He's just as bad. You watch. He'll keep being Ben's

friend. So will Adrian and the other guy. They'll laugh about it. That's what guys do."

"Not me."

"Not you."

We each took a candle and made our way down the passage to the entrance. A little piece of me was sorry to be going—I felt like something good had happened with me and Gaia—but mostly I was hungry for open sky.

I climbed the steel gate. It was still light out. I was surprised, like when you come out of a movie matinee and expect it to be dark but the sun is shining. I felt as if we'd wandered those dark passageways for ten hours. I reached down and helped Gaia up, and moments later we were standing outside.

The Mustang was the only car there.

"At least they didn't slash my tires," I said, then noticed the long, deep scratch across the passenger side. One of them had keyed the door.

I stared at the damage, thinking at least it was on the passenger side. When I parked the car in the garage, Mom wouldn't see the scratch.

We didn't talk much on the way home. I was surprised when Gaia grabbed my hand and held it. I drove all the way with just my left hand on the wheel. She kept looking at me and not saying anything. That side of my face felt warm, as if her eyes were heat lamps.

When I signaled to turn onto Ash Avenue, Gaia squeezed my fingers and said, "Can we go to your house?"

"Okay." I stayed on the boulevard and a few minutes later pulled into my driveway. I hopped out and rolled up the garage door. Gaia watched me from the passenger seat.

"You'd better climb out here," I said. "It's kind of tight inside."

She got out. I pulled into the garage. The side with the scratch was inches from the stacks of cases from Sam's Club. Mom would never see it. Probably.

Gaia followed me into the garage. We squeezed between the car and the cases and went through the connecting door into the kitchen.

"Thirsty?" I asked. We hadn't had anything to drink for what seemed like hours.

"God, yes!"

I grabbed some waters from the fridge. We plopped down onto the sofa and guzzled them as if we'd been lost in the desert for days.

"Well," I said, "that was fun."

Gaia had sat down really close to me, so our shoulders were pressed together.

"I thought you were lost and I'd never see you again," she said.

"Me too."

"You were trying to find me."

"I was scared something had happened to you."

"Those fireworks went off, and I sort of freaked."

"Me too."

"I'm sorry. I shouldn't have run off."

"It's okay."

She said, "So your mom is gone till tomorrow?"

"Yeah, she's at some yoga retreat, sweating."

I could smell my own sweat, layered with hours of walking and fear. Gaia leaned her head on my shoulder.

"I bet I stink," I said. I could smell her too. I liked it.

"You smell good." She turned her head and kissed me on the cheek. "You're bristly."

"I shave," I said. Okay, once every three or four days.

She drew back slightly and ran her fingers softly across my jaw. I could feel each whisker bend and spring back at her passing touch. I turned to look at her. Her eyes were moving, exploring my face, shifting rapidly. Her pupils were enormous.

She said, "Can we go to your room?"

# "300 Pounds of Joy"

## Howlin' Wolf
## 3:12

**I'm sitting on a bench across from the Mark** Twain Boyhood Home and Museum. A man is pretending to paint "Tom Sawyer's fence" while his wife takes pictures with her phone. I go back to studying my Great River Road map. I could cross the river here, which would get me out of Missouri and into Illinois. It'll be dark in a couple of hours. I don't want to sleep in my car again, and I could really use a shower. Stay in Missouri or head for Illinois? Saint Louis is too far, and besides, big cities make me nervous. I'd like to find a little motel off the beaten path. Illinois or Missouri?

I'm pondering that when I'm startled by a sudden tremor. For a split second I think, *Earthquake!* Then I realize that an exceptionally large man has plonked down on the other end of the bench. He tugs a paisley kerchief from the breast pocket of his overalls and wipes his forehead.

"You know what this town needs?" he asks me.

*A bulldozer*, I think. But I don't say that. I just shrug and go back to looking at my map.

"Golf carts," the man says.

"Golf carts?" I say.

"Yeah. Like they have at Disney."

"They have golf carts at Disney?" I say. I have no idea what he's talking about.

"For the physically challenged. The disabled. Ride around in comfort. That's what they need here. Golf carts."

"Are you disabled?" I ask.

He makes a *poof* sound with his lips and says, "Christ, look at me!"

He has a point. The guy can't be more than forty years old, but his face is slick with perspiration, and I bet he's four hundred pounds. I wonder how he ties his shoes. I look down. His shoes are slip-ons.

"I used to be a skinny kid just like you. Two-thirty when I graduated high school."

"I only weigh *one*-thirty," I tell him.

"Yeah, well, ain't you something. You got a girl-friend?"

I don't know why he would ask me that. I shake my head and go back to looking at the map. I can hear him breathing.

"So what do you think of this," he says, gesturing. "Tom Sawyer's fence. Quite the deal."

"Tom Sawyer never existed," I say.

The man gives me a long look and shakes his head.

"You got no romance in you, kid."

"I have romance."

"Whatever you say." The man rocks back and throws his bulk forward to stand. He makes it to his feet. For a moment I think he is going to come crashing back down, possibly shattering the wooden bench, but he catches his balance. "Got to check out that fence," he says, and lumbers off.

# Tennis Balls

**Garf gaped.**

"You did it?" he said.

I instantly felt like a complete and total ass. But I'd had to tell *somebody*, and Garf was all I had.

It was nine o'clock in the morning, and we were in his backyard throwing tennis balls at a bucket. Neither of us played tennis, but Garf's brother Jimmy had, when he was alive. Garf had found a whole laundry basket full of used tennis balls in his basement.

"Yeah, we did it," I said. I threw a ball and missed. The bucket was all the way on the other side of the lawn against the fence. We'd thrown a dozen balls and hadn't gotten one in yet.

Garf threw another ball. Missed.

"So you're, like, not in the club anymore?"

"What club is that?"

"The virgin club!"

"Garf, goddammit!" I threw a ball, hard. It bounced off the rim of the bucket and went straight up over the fence.

"I'm just saying," Garf said.

"You're just an idiot."

"Yeah, well, I know that. So . . . ?"

"So that's all." I wished I'd never said anything.

"Dude, I need details! This is the most momentous thing that's ever happened in your entire life!"

"Momentous?" I thought about my dad dying.

"I remember my first time," he said.

"You?" Nothing else he could have said would have surprised me more.

"Yeah, it was my cousin Kelsey. I mean, she's my mom's cousin's daughter, so it's not like she's actually that close of a relative. She's a couple years older than me."

"How old were you?"

"It was last year, just after my brother died. Just the one time." He shrugged. "It was her idea. I mean, she sort of seduced me, I guess. I think she felt sorry for me. Or something. So . . . where were you?"

"Forget I said anything," I said.

We had been in my bedroom. Gaia had looked around, then started turning all my Darth Vader figures so they faced the wall. I'd just stood and watched, not sure what to do. When she'd turned the last Vader, she looked at me, very serious.

"Okay?" she said.

"What about Wonder Woman?"

"She can watch."

A second later we were kissing, our tongues filling each other's mouths, our breaths coming in gasps, our smell so strong and bestial I thought I would sink and drown in it and never come up again. There were no words. Clothes came off and my entire body melted.

There was no way I would—or could—tell any of that to Garf. It was mine. Mine and Gaia's.

After, we lay on my bed, her leg crossed over mine, my arm under her head, heat rising off our sweaty, naked bodies. I turned my head and looked at her, the most beautiful creature I had ever seen, and wondered, *How did I get here*?

She was the first one to speak.

"Well," she said.

"Well, what?"

She didn't reply.

We lay there like that for an hour. I kept remembering every detail; I never wanted to forget. I was already thinking about the next time. Was she thinking the same thing? I hoped I'd done everything okay. I thought it was okay. Did she think so? I was just happy to be there with her, our skin touching, our breath filling the air.

I wanted to stay there with her forever. Or at least all night.

"My mom won't be home until tomorrow," I said.

"I have to get home."

I looked at the clock. Nine thirty. It was still a little light out. I heard a distant boom.

"The fireworks are just starting," I said.

"I told you what I think about fireworks. Anyway, my dad will freak if I'm not home by ten."

"Text him. Tell him you're staying at Maeve's."

"My dad doesn't text. He doesn't even have a cell."

I think that's when I realized that I knew nothing about Gaia Nygren.

I knew she had a brother, of course—the over-achieving Derek—although he was a year ahead of me and I didn't really know him. I knew she lived in a white rambler on Ash Avenue. I knew she lived with her dad, who drove a Subaru and taught at the U, but I'd never met him and knew nothing about him. She never said anything about her mother. I had the feeling she wasn't around anymore. I knew Gaia was a year younger than me; I knew her birthday was in October. I knew her phone number. I knew her body.

But I had no idea what her life was like when she wasn't with me. She didn't talk about it. I never asked. I was afraid to. I liked to think of her as unconnected, unburdened.

"I should go." She sat up. She stood up. Watching

her putting her clothes on was just as sexy as watching them come off.

"What does he teach? Your dad, I mean."

"Art history."

I waited for more, but it didn't come.

"What about your mom?"

"They got divorced."

"Oh." I was embarrassed that I hadn't known that.

"She lives in Santa Fe."

"Sorry. Um . . . how come you live with your dad and not with her?"

"She left."

"Oh. Why?"

"She said she had to *find* herself." She snorted out a laugh. "She's an *artist*. Whatever. It was a year ago."

"That must have been hard. I mean, for you."

"It's not like she was this great mom."

I didn't know what to say to that.

"She said it was either us or her life. She was all about making choices. She chose to move to New Mexico and make her stupid paintings. She calls every now and then. She says I should come and visit, but I don't want to."

"You're pretty mad at her?"

"What do you think?"

"I'm mad at my dad."

"Yeah, I know."

"I guess he made a choice too."

"I should go."

I pulled on my jeans and grabbed a T-shirt. We went downstairs. There were things I felt I should be saying, but everything I thought of sounded lame: *You are beautiful. That was fun. I love you.*

I didn't say anything. We went out to the garage and got in the Mustang, and I drove her home, trying to understand how we could have been so incredibly close a few minutes before, yet now I sensed a gulf between us. Had I done something? Said something? Was it because I hadn't known that her mom was gone?

When we got to her house, I leaned over to kiss her, and she kissed me back, but it wasn't the same.

"See you," she said, and got out of the car.

"See you," I said back.

So lame.


I could tell that Garf was disappointed because I wouldn't talk about it, but he shrugged it off.

"Did you call her yet?" he asked. We had thrown all the tennis balls. They were scattered all over the yard.

"What do you mean?"

"You're supposed to call the next morning."

"I texted her."

"Did she text back?"

I dug my phone out of my pocket and checked.

"Not yet."

"Did you use a rubber?"

I gave him my *How stupid do you think I am?* look and said, "Duh."

# "Dream Lover"

## Bobby Darin
## 2:32

**An hour south of Hannibal, on the Illinois** side of the river, I pull into a motel called Dreaming Pines. I see no pine trees, but it looks like the sort of place where they won't care how old I am or whose credit card I'm using. The old guy at the desk is fixated on a baseball game playing on the lobby TV. He's wearing a Saint Louis Cardinals cap.

"Who's playing?" I ask to get his attention.

"Cards and Cubbies at Busch," he says without looking at me.

"What's 'Busch'?" I ask.

Now he looks at me, as if he cannot believe I would ask such a question. "It's the Cards' stadium," he says. "Home game."

"Oh. Can I get a room?"

He sighs, stands, and pushes a form across the counter. "Name, license number, how many nights. Visa, Mastercard, or cash." He goes back to watching the game. I fill in the blanks and take out my mom's card. He runs it through his machine without looking at it and a few seconds later gives me a key.

"Checkout time's eleven," he says.

"Is there someplace to eat around here?" I ask.

He points at a vending machine at the side of the lobby. I examine the delicacies on offer. Candy and various greasy salty things. I pump money into the machine until I have a meal: Fritos, a granola bar, pretzels, and peanut M&M's. I buy a Mountain Dew from a different machine outside.

Room number 112 is at the end. The carpet is worn, the fake-wood-paneled walls are scratched, the mattress is uneven, and it smells like some cheap cleaning product with a faint tang of body odor, but to me it looks like heaven. I throw myself onto the bed and stare up at the stained ceiling tiles. I am so tired; I can feel tiredness leaking out through my pores. I've only been gone for two days. It feels like forever. I think about turning on the TV. Cards versus Cubs? No, thank you. I think about calling my mom, just to tell her not to worry. There's a phone on the bedside table. She'd take a collect call, probably, but no, I can't hear her voice, whether it's the angry voice, the whiny voice, or some other voice that makes me feel like a piece of crap.

I eat Fritos and M&M's and think about going back out to the car and getting the map so I can see where the Great River Road will take me.

Instead I fall asleep.

# Nailed

**After I left Garf's, I stopped at Walgreens.**
There were a lot of kinds of condoms. I'd heard of
Trojans, so I bought a pack of those. When I got
home, Mom's car was in the driveway. She was in the
kitchen cleaning up my breakfast mess.

"Hey," I said.

She answered by putting my cereal bowl in the
dishwasher and slamming the door shut.

"Sorry," I said. "I was going to clean up."

"Did you have a nice *trip*?" she asked, still not looking at me.

I said, "Trip?"

She turned, her back to the counter, her eyes drill-
ing into me.

"Trip," she said.

I tried to look innocent, but my thoughts were churning. I'm sure I looked guilty as hell.

"Do you know what Marnie Matthews said to me?" Mrs. Matthews was the busybody old lady who lived across the street from us.

"How would I know that?" I said. It was the wrong thing to say. Her face hardened.

"She said you drove off in your father's car yesterday morning."

"Oh." I scrambled. "Yeah, I did. Just a quick trip around the neighborhood. It's not good for it to just sit in the garage."

"She said you were gone all day."

I shrugged. Nailed. I waited for the next thing, and when it came, I wasn't ready for it: she started crying.

"Mom . . ."

"Leave me alone!" She walked, stiff-legged, out of the kitchen. Seconds later I heard her bedroom door slam.

I felt bad. Guilty, ashamed, and foolish. That didn't last long, though, because I started to get mad. The Mustang was *my* car. It was just *sitting* in the garage. And she'd left me here with no other transportation available. Was I supposed to sit around and watch TV the whole time she was de-stressing at yoga camp? Did she even ask me if it was okay if she went? And why was she *crying*? So selfish. It was all about her. Never mind what I needed. Never mind that I had a life of my own. I was almost seventeen, and she was still treating me like I was seven. . . .

. . . And then I felt guilty and ashamed all over again because her *husband* had died, and I thought how I would feel if Gaia died. . . .

. . . And then I got mad because Dad was my *dad*. She'd had him for twenty-five years, and for me it was only sixteen years and five months. She was an adult. She was supposed to be the grown-up, and now she was crying and hiding in her room. It wasn't fair.

I could hear my dad saying that. *It's not fair.* He had said it a lot, sometimes resignedly, shaking his head, sometimes in anger. *What a crock!* It wasn't fair that he got blamed for the forklift accident. It wasn't fair that he didn't get paid more. It wasn't fair that life sucks and then you die.

It wasn't fair that he killed himself.

I needed Gaia. I checked my phone for the hundredth time. No text back. I called her number. Five rings, then her voice mail. I didn't leave a message. All I wanted was to hear her voice.

I thought about taking the Mustang again since I was in trouble anyway, but Mom had blocked the garage door with her Toyota. I set out on foot. Gaia lived three miles away.

On the way there I kept checking my phone. Nothing. Nada. Zilch. I thought of all the reasons why she maybe hadn't called me back: lost phone, sleeping late, busy doing something else, mad at me, hates me. Why would she hate me? She always said I was too negative. But she was the one with the *Life Sucks* T-shirt and the sullen expression. And if she hated me, then why had we done what we did? How could she hate someone who wanted her so much? I hadn't even showered that morning because I didn't want to wash her off me.

I pulled out the neck of my tee and sniffed. Not bad, but they say you can't smell your own stink.

# "Frownland"
## Captain Beefheart
## 1:42

**Breakfast is Fritos, pretzels, and a Styro-**foam cup of coffee from the motel lobby. I have showered and changed into a fresh pair of jeans and a polo shirt that used to be my dad's. The day is bright and pleasantly cool. I drive with the windows down, listening to a random mix from Dad's iPod. The Rolling Stones, Courtney Love, Iggy Pop, Snoop Dogg. Dad had some seriously weird tastes. Roxy Music and Radiohead. James Taylor and Miley Cyrus. *Hannah Montana?* Weird.

I wish we'd talked about music more. I wish we'd talked about music at *all*. He never listened to it at home, just in his car, by himself, alone. I knew him my whole life and had no idea. It was almost as if I never knew him at all.

I drive south, trying to imagine him when he was my age. What kind of music was he listening to then? I don't know much about eighties music. It was after the Beatles and the Stones, before Nirvana, and before hip-hop got big. I scroll through the iPod, keeping one eye on the road. Sex Pistols? Journey? Were they eighties?

I hear my dad in my head, yelling at me, *Put the iPod down and drive! You want to get us both killed?*

I put the iPod down.

Saint Louis is on the Missouri side of the river. I don't want to deal with big-city traffic, so I stay on the Illinois side. The road takes me through Grafton, Elsah, and Alton, following the river closely for once. South of Alton I miss a turn and end up in a place called Pontoon Beach, where I see neither pontoons nor beaches. It's almost noon, so I stop at a Burger King and order a Whopper with fries and a Coke. They take Mom's credit card. I really should call her. But if she wants to know I'm still alive, she can always check the charges on her card.

I sit in the car and look at the Great River Road map as I eat. The "points of interest" triangles don't look very interesting—mostly museums and such. I notice one place called Cahokia Mounds State Historic Site. It's only a few miles away. I look through the various brochures I've picked up and find one about Cahokia. The brochure is pretty interesting. I'm still sitting in the BK parking lot reading it after my last french fry is gone.

Cahokia, according to the brochure, was home to the Mississippians, a Native American culture that lived along the Mississippi and its tributaries. As many as forty thousand Mississippians once lived in and around Cahokia. Their civilization collapsed in the 1400s; nobody knows why. Maybe flooding, or droughts, or politics, or who knows what. When the European explorers arrived in the 1500s, they brought smallpox and other diseases, and that pretty much wiped out what was left of the civilization. The Mississippians are gone now, but they left about eighty mounds behind, including the biggest earthen mound in the Americas.

There are Indian mounds all over the Midwest— I saw some in Minnesota. They just look like hills. I guess if you dig into them, you can find pottery and bones and stuff, but you're not supposed to do that.

The biggest mound at Cahokia is called Monks Mound, even though no monks were involved in its construction. It's *huge*. The whole thing was built by hand, one basket of dirt at a time. I want to see that mound.

The road takes me past a big lake. I still don't see any beaches or pontoons, but there could be some. Almost as soon as I'm past the lake, I see a sign for the Cahokia Mounds. I turn, and off to the left I see the big mound.

It doesn't look all that big.

I drive past the mound and join half a dozen other cars in the parking area. The mound looks bigger from here, like a pyramid with its top lopped off and its edges worn smooth. A crushed gravel path leads from the parking lot toward the south side of the mound. Along the way there are signs with information about the site, including some paintings of what life was like for the Mississippians way back when. The artist makes it look utterly peaceful and idyllic. I'm sure those Indians had to deal with a lot of their own assholes even before the assholes from Europe arrived and brought smallpox with them, but the paintings make it look like a nice place to live.

One of the signs says that there used to be a hundred and fifty mounds, but only half of them remain. I can see a few of the smaller mounds, like little hills where you wouldn't expect to find a hill. The gravel crunches under my feet, and the big mound keeps getting bigger, and for a few seconds I feel as if I'm in a dream. Then I see a crumpled cigarette pack on the path, and the dream feeling goes away. Some asshole. I kick it off to the side. A few steps later I stop and go back and pick it up and put it in my pocket. I'll get rid of it next time I see a trash can.

A wooden stairway leads up the side of the mound. I count the steps as I climb. After sixty steps I reach a flat area, a sort of terrace about a hundred feet across. I suppose it could have been a place where you could rest your legs, or maybe a Mississippian food court where they served roasted rabbits or corn on the cob. Not sure what they ate back then. There's nothing here now, not even a trash can for the cigarette packet in my pocket.

The steps continue. I don't count them, but there must be another hundred at least. When I finally reach the top, I see that I'm not alone.

# Benches

**I pressed the doorbell and heard a faint** chime from inside. The door opened. Derek, Gaia's older brother.

I have mentioned Derek before—student council president, tall, blond, good-looking, friendly, etc., etc., etc. Straight out of central casting for some cookie-cutter teen drama on TV.

"Hey, Stiggy," he said. He knew my name because if he hadn't, he wouldn't have been so absurdly perfect. He probably knew the names of all two thousand students at Saint Andrew Valley High School. "What's up?"

"Is Gaia around?"

A light went on behind his long-lashed blue eyes.

"Oh! You're the guy she won't talk about?"

"I don't know who she doesn't talk about," I said, which had sounded great in my head before it'd dribbled out of my mouth.

"Come on in," he said.

I stepped inside. It looked like every other three-bedroom suburban rambler I'd been in. Carpeted living room off to the right with a sofa facing the picture window, coat closet on the left, pictures on the walls, a short hallway leading to what I assumed was the kitchen. The house had the odd, nose-tweaking smell of athletic deodorant—then I realized it was Derek. His hair was damp. I deduced that he'd just gotten out of the shower and slathered himself with something.

"Guy!" he yelled over his shoulder. I thought for a second he was announcing my arrival, but quickly figured out that "Guy" was short for "Gaia." I bet she hated it.

"What?" Gaia's voice coming from the kitchen.

"You have a gentleman caller."

Gaia appeared in the hallway holding a plastic bowl of cereal and a spoon. She was wearing gray sweat-pants and a plain white T-shirt. Her hair was pulled back in a ponytail, and her face looked scrubbed. No earrings. I'd never seen her without makeup.

"Stiggy," she said. I couldn't tell if she was surprised, pleased, disappointed, or bored.

"Hi," I said.

"Let me put this down." She went back to the

kitchen. I heard the clunk of the bowl dropping into the sink. I noticed a photo propped on a side table, a picture of two kids in swimsuits standing on a dock. Gaia returned, wiping her palms on her sweatpants.

"That's me and Derek up at the lake," she said.

Derek was still standing there in the hallway, watching us with a little smirk.

"So are you guys an item?" he said.

Gaia gave him a withering look that she'd probably given him a thousand times before. Derek grinned, shrugged, and wandered off to apply another layer of Manly Stank or whatever it was.

Gaia smiled. She held her hands out to the side and said, "Welcome to the American Dream made manifest."

That sounded like a quote, but I didn't know what from.

She grinned and said, "That's what my dad calls our house."

"I texted you," I said.

"Oh. Yeah. I was over at Maeve's and forgot my phone here."

"How's Maeve?" I didn't really care.

"She's a mess. You want to go sit out back?"

I nodded, then followed her through the kitchen and out the sliding patio doors to the backyard. A back garden, really. Instead of a lawn like everybody else had, the yard was all brick-edged plantings. A flagstone path wove between the rosebushes and peony beds.

"My dad's kind of anal about his yard."

She led me down the path to where three curved stone benches faced one another. We sat down on the ends of adjacent benches. About twelve inches separated our knees. I had never been more attracted to her.

"You look amazing," I said. She smiled, and I knew that for once I had said exactly the right thing. Then I added, "Even better without the makeup." Which was exactly the wrong thing, apparently.

"Thanks a lot," she said, looking abruptly distant. She was good at that.

"You look great with makeup too," I said quickly.

She gave a small nod and studied the rosebush over my shoulder.

"I thought maybe we could do something tonight," I said. "Except I won't have a car. My nosy neighbor told my mom I took the Mustang, so she's kind of pissed. But I don't know, maybe walk over to the Heights?" The Heights was a little movie theater where they showed old movies. My parents used to go there a couple of times a month to watch movies from when they were kids. *Date night*, they called it.

Gaia said, "What's showing?"

I didn't know. It didn't matter to me. Why did it matter to her?

She saw my disappointment and shrugged. "Sure," she said. "Whatever."

"Or we could do something else."

"No, a movie's fine."

O O O

Back at home, things had not warmed up. My mom was giving me the silent treatment. For dinner she had made herself a grilled cheese, but she didn't make one for me. She took it to the den and turned on PBS and ate by herself; I had to make my own sandwich. At least she hadn't tried to ground me. We both knew that wouldn't work.

I left on foot, and got to Gaia's around seven thirty. The movie was at eight. Gaia's dad was home, but I didn't have to go inside. She saw me coming and met me on the sidewalk. She was back in her uniform. Black jeans, black sneakers, and black top, with mascara and dark eyebrows, and lipstick the color of sunburn. Same with her fingernails.

"What are we seeing?" she asked.

"*Fargo*," I said. "And they're showing *Rocky Horror* at midnight."

"Ugh. No, thanks."

"No *Fargo*?"

"No, *Fargo*'s fine. I've never seen it. But no *Rocky Horror*, please. I've seen it, like, six times. Anyway, my dad would freak if I stayed out till two in the morning."

The theater was a mile away. We'd only gone a couple of blocks when she said, "I don't want to sit in a movie theater. It's nice out. Let's just walk."

"Okay."

"We could do the River Walk."

"All of it?" The River Walk was a hiking path that

ran for miles along the Mississippi. I'd been on it a few times.

"Just however much we feel like," she said.

We walked. Gaia was talking about Maeve. I was only half listening. I liked hearing her talk, though. I could feel her voice not just in my ears but all over my body.

Gaia poked me with her elbow. "Did you hear what I said?"

"Sorry. What?"

"She found him."

"Who found who?"

"Maeve found Michael! Her *boyfriend*? Who's been missing for over a *month*? Turns out he's staying at Maeve's uncle's farm in Prairie du Chien."

"He's at her cool organic uncle's cool organic farm?"

"He's been there the whole time. Only, he doesn't want anybody except Maeve to know, so don't tell anybody."

"Who would I tell?"

"Just don't. Anyway, Maeve's going down there. Like, to live."

"On a farm?"

"She wants to finish high school in Prairie du Chien. Her mom is cool with it."

"Her mom's cool that Maeve's going to live with her boyfriend?"

"Things haven't been so good for her at home. I think her mom's just glad to be rid of her."

That made me think of my mom. What would she

do if I told her Gaia and I were going to live on a farm in Wisconsin? She'd totally freak out—or would she? I could also imagine her sighing with relief to be rid of her cranky car-stealing son. I really didn't know what she'd do. Gaia was still talking, but I wasn't really listening. I was glad Maeve was moving. I wanted Gaia all to myself.

We were almost to the river when she said, "So?"

"So, what?"

"So, what do you think? About what I've been saying?"

"Great," I said. "That's great." It seemed like a safe response since I hadn't heard a word in the last five minutes.

"Great?" She stopped walking and put her hands on her hips. "Maeve's life is a complete disaster, and you think that's great?"

*Oh shit.*

"I mean, I think it's great that you're telling me all this," I said.

She rolled her eyes in that very Gaia way and started walking again. I fell in beside her and tried a new tack.

"Speaking of Maeve . . . did you tell her about us?"

"Tell her what?" She was irritated with me, I could tell.

"That we . . . um . . ." I almost said "made love," but that sounded corny. I almost said "had sex," but that was too clinical.

"Did it?" Gaia said.

Okay, that was another way to put it.

"Yeah," I said.

"Of course I told her. She's my friend."

"So I should tell all my friends?"

"No!"

"What if I told Garf?"

"Garf Neff? Are you kidding me? The very thought of you and me having sex inside Garf Neff's sick little mind is totally barf-inducing."

"Garf's not so bad."

"Whatever."

She was in a mood, and I didn't understand why, so we walked without talking for a while. We reached the path along the river, a sort of wooded trail with a steep bank dropping off to our right and the river visible through the treetops. The path dipped down, a long stairway made of rough-cut logs and packed dirt. We went all the way down to the river and out onto a little sandy spit. It would have been pretty, except for all the trash washed up on the shore. We stood there for a while and watched a tugboat pushing a barge downriver.

"I wonder where they go," Gaia said.

"The summer after high school, my dad and my uncle Donny bought a canoe. They wanted to paddle down the river all the way to New Orleans."

"That sounds romantic."

"It wasn't. They only got as far as Winona. Donny

was swatting at a horsefly, and the canoe tipped over in the middle of the river. They lost all their gear, and the canoe got away from them." It was a story Dad had told many times, especially the part about it being Donny's fault that they'd capsized. "They had to swim to shore and hitchhike home."

Gaia gave me an accusing look. "You always end your stories on a downer."

"That's what happened!"

"You don't have to tell it that way."

"I don't know another way to tell it."

She looked away, out over the water.

"It's hard, isn't it?" I could barely hear her.

"What? Canoeing?"

"Relationships. Telling things. Being honest."

"I'm always honest."

"Sometimes I wish you weren't."

"You want me to lie more?"

"I want you to lie just enough."

We continued along the path and came to another long set of stairs, going up.

The sun was almost gone. I was getting an anxious feeling deep in my gut, and I wasn't sure why. It wasn't because Gaia was cranky or because it would be dark soon—it was something else. We followed the stairs back and forth, a zigzag up the bluff, and emerged into a large grassy park. I knew then what was making me uneasy.

"Where are we?" Gaia asked.

"East River Park," I said.

There were benches, four metal benches painted blue, where you could sit and look out over the flowing waters. Or look, as my father had done on that cold February afternoon, at the frozen river. I wondered if he'd thought about paddling down the river with Donny, heading for the Gulf, before putting the shotgun to his neck and pulling the trigger.

Which bench, though?

"Let's sit down for a while," Gaia said.

"No," I said.

# "Wolverton Mountain"

## Claude King
## 2:38

**Monks Mound is nearly a hundred feet tall.**
It used to be higher, but over the past five hundred years the land has filled in around the base, and the top has worn down. It was once covered with wooden buildings, but they're long gone. Now the top is just a flat, grassy rectangle, big enough for a game of soccer if you don't mind losing a lot of balls over the edge.

A family—mom, dad, and two little kids—is standing a few yards from the top of the stairs. Dad is taking pictures with his phone. That's what my dad would've done. They ignore me. I walk past them, following a path leading to the west edge of the mound. I can see Saint Louis. I can see the Gateway Arch glinting in the sun. It must be ten or fifteen miles away. I wonder if the tourists in the arch can see Cahokia.

The only other people on the mound are at the far end. Three of them. They look about my age. I follow the path and eventually pass near them. It's two guys and a girl. One of the guys is sitting on an overstuffed backpack playing with his dreadlocks. He's blond. I don't get it—why would a white guy want dreads? He's wearing a serape, giving his Rasta pretentions a Mexican twist. The other guy has kind of an angry vibe. He has lank brown hair down past his scowl, a couple weeks of scraggly beard, a fake-looking tie-dye shirt, and a cigarette hanging out of the corner of his mouth.

The girl is taking selfies with the two guys in the background. She's wearing a Bob Marley tee, which makes me wonder if the dreadlocked guy is her boyfriend. Her hair is a big mop of curly reddish blond, and her face is freckled. She lowers her phone and smiles at me.

"Hey," I say.

"Hi!" She has a cheerful voice—the kind of voice that usually bugs me, but it's been a while since I've talked to anybody my age, so I'm glad to hear it. "Where did you come from?"

"He's a Cake," the angry guy says.

"What's a Cake?" I ask. The way he said it makes me think it's an insult.

He takes a drag off his cigarette and flicks it away. "Perfect Village," he says.

I look at the girl, who is smiling. "I don't know why Bran said that," she says.

"'Cause of his shirt," Bran says.

I look down to see what I'm wearing. It's one of my dad's polo shirts, with a little penguin embroidered on the chest. He used to wear it a lot.

"This is what they wear in Perfect Village?" I ask, wondering if that's a real place or just something he made up.

"Don't pay any attention to him." The girl walks closer to me and peers into my face. Her eyes are intensely blue. "You're cute," she says.

"Allie is known for her crap taste in guys," says Bran.

The faux Rasta laughs. He's messing with his hair, twisting the end of a lock between his fingers.

"Are you guys from around here?" I ask.

"Yeah, we're ancient Cahokians, Cake," says Bran.

"How come he keeps calling me 'Cake'?" I ask Allie.

"Bran has an attitude. He's working on his self-loathing."

Bran scowls loathingly.

"What's your name?" she asks.

"Stiggy."

"Where are you from?"

"Minnesota. I'm just driving through."

"Minnesota! Brrr!" says Allie.

"It's actually not that cold. Except sometimes."

"You got a car?" Bran asks.

"Uh . . . yeah?"

Bran and the faux Rasta look at each other.

Bran makes a face that I think is supposed to be a smile. "Maybe you could give us a lift?"

"You don't have a car? How'd you get here?" I ask.

"We walked," says Allie. "We have a camp up at Horseshoe."

That's the name of the big lake I passed a couple of miles back.

"We were going into Fairmont for supplies," she says. "But Randy wanted to check out the mounds." Randy must be the guy with the dreads.

"There's a Foodland just up the road," Bran says.

"You just want a ride to the store?" I ask. I'm looking them over, trying to figure out if they're dangerous. I don't think so—just a couple of doofuses and a pretty girl.

Bran nods. "And maybe a ride from there back to Horseshoe?"

I look at Allie, who isn't saying anything. She smiles and nods.

I pull into a parking space in the Foodland parking lot. Randy and Bran get out of the back and head into the store. Allie, in the passenger seat, stays.

"They know what to get," she says.

"Those guys are a little ripe."

"That's just Randy. He doesn't believe in soap."

"So you guys are just . . . camping out?"

"For now. We're headed south. There's a Renaissance Festival in Louisiana. Randy juggles. I do food service. Bran does whatever. But the RenFest isn't for another few weeks, so we're hanging out until then."

"You don't have to go to school or anything?"

"I'm done with that. I did a year at KCAI. That's where I met Randy."

"Is that a radio station?"

She laughs. "It's an art college. Kansas City Art Institute."

"Oh, of course." I'm surprised. She must be a couple of years older than me. Now I feel like a kid. "Is Randy your boyfriend?"

"He was, sort of. Now we're just friends." She kicks off her sandals and puts her bare feet on the dash. Her toenails used to be green, but there are only a few chips of polish left on them. "Do you have a girlfriend?"

"No." I say it louder than I meant to, and she sort of flinches. "Not at the moment," I add.

She nods, as if all is explained.

"Randy and I have been camping since June. Bran hooked up with us a few weeks ago at a festival up in Iowa." She gives me a side glance. "What about you?"

"I'm driving down the river road," I say.

"All by yourself?"

I nod, then feel the need to explain myself. "Things sucked back home. I'm taking some time off."

"I get that. Do you have family back in Minnesota?"

I think about my mom, and my dad.

"Just my mom," I say.

"I hear you. Maybe things will be better when you go back."

"If I go back."

She smiles at her feet but doesn't say anything.

I hear a shout and look up. Randy and Bran are running toward the car, pushing a cart piled high with groceries. A bag of potato chips flies off the top; neither of them look back.

"Open the door!" Bran yells.

Allie pushes open her door and pulls her seatback forward. Randy and Bran start throwing stuff from the cart into the backseat: more chips, hot dogs, a bag of oranges, a carton of Marlboros, two six-packs of beer, a loaf of bread, and a bunch of other stuff. A man wearing a green apron comes running out of the store. Randy and Bran pile into the backseat on top of all the groceries.

"Go!" Bran yells. The guy in the apron is only about two seconds from reaching us. He looks really mad. Allie slams the door, and I hit the gas. The Mustang lurches forward. As we pull away, the guy punches the passenger-side window so hard, I'm amazed it doesn't break. I almost crash into a cart corral but miss it by inches.

Bran and Randy are laughing hysterically.

"Did you *see* that guy?" Bran says. "What an asshole! Did you *see* him?"

I hit the parking lot exit going about forty.

"Left! Go left!" Bran yells.

We screech onto Collinsville Road. My heart is pounding. Allie is turned around in her seat yelling at Randy. "You didn't tell me you were going to do that!"

"What?" Bran says. "Did we forget something?"

Allie spins back in her seat and crosses her arms. "You didn't have to. We're not broke."

"Yet," says Randy.

"Hey, we just saved about a hundred bucks." Bran thrusts a yellow bag between our seats. "We got Funyuns!"

Allie shakes her head. "I didn't know they were going to do that." She smiles. I can't tell if she's embarrassed, apologetic, or just happy about the Funyuns.

# Benches 2

**You never know what people are going to do.**
I didn't know my dad was going to kill himself. I
didn't know Gaia was going to leave me. My whole
life was people doing things I never dreamed of.
Including myself. I'd never dreamed I'd be the getaway driver in a grocery-store heist, for example.

The night that Gaia and I went for that long walk
and ended up in East River Park, where my dad had
killed himself—I didn't know I was going to be such
a jerk. I keep going back to it, wondering if that was
the beginning of the end for Gaia and me. I mean, I
really was a jerk.

She just wanted to sit on a bench and look out over
the river. And I wouldn't do it.

"Why not?" she asked.

It was a reasonable question. I should have told her. I wanted to. She would have understood.

"I don't feel like sitting." I said it kind of mean. There was a storm in my head. I wanted to break something. I wanted to break every bench in the park.

"Well, *I* do." Her confusion was turning to anger.

"Fine. Sit. I'm leaving." I turned away from her and started walking.

"Stiggy!" she yelled after me.

I kept walking. Gaia ran to catch up. She grabbed my arm.

"What's the matter with you?" she asked.

"Nothing." I just couldn't tell her about my dad. I mean, she knew that he'd killed himself. Everybody did. But I just couldn't tell her he'd done it there, maybe on that bench not fifty feet from where we were standing. It was too close, too real.

The feelings I had about my dad were all mixed up. They included sadness, of course. And anger, and loneliness, and this miserable barfy feeling that always came when I thought about it too much. But the worst one was shame. I was ashamed of Dad for giving up, and ashamed of myself for not knowing, for not being able to help. Ashamed of being his son, ashamed of not being the son he'd needed.

I couldn't stand for Gaia to see me being that person, so instead of explaining myself, I kept walking. She followed—it was getting darker, and I'm sure she didn't want to be out there all alone—and tried to talk to me, but all I heard was the noise in my head. After a while she stopped trying and simply followed. I could hear her footsteps about ten feet behind me. I didn't say anything until we were almost to her house.

My internal shit-storm had subsided by then— enough for me to say, "Sorry."

"Nice walk," she said shortly. I watched her walk up to her front door and let herself in.

Two hours later, after replaying things over and over in my head, I texted her an apology.

**Don't worry about it,** she texted back.

I guessed she was awake thinking about things too.

# "I Put a Spell on You"

## Nina Simone
## 2:39

**We park in a public lot at the eastern side of** Horseshoe Lake. Bran and Randy get out and start stuffing all the stolen groceries into their backpacks. I see a canned ham, a bag of apples, boxes of crackers, a tray of Oreos, two loaves of bread, a can of sardines, a big bag of ice, and all sorts of other stuff. Hard to believe it all fit in the car.

"We have to walk in," Allie says.

"Our camp is kind of illegal," Bran adds with a laugh.

"You want to come check it out?" Allie asks me. "We're out on Walker's Island."

"Also, we could use a hand carrying all this crap," Bran says. "Here, Cake. You can carry this." Bran tosses me a ten-pound bag of ice.

We hike across a short causeway onto the island and follow a trail through an open field. The ice is freezing my fingers; I have to keep moving it from one arm to the other.

On the far side of the island, the trail enters a wooded area. About fifty yards off the trail in a small, grassy clearing are two nylon tents partially covered with leafy branches, a fire pit with a grill made out of an old box spring, a picnic table, and a large red plastic cooler.

"Home sweet home," Bran says. He takes the ice from me and puts it into the cooler, along with two six-packs of beer and a few other things from his backpack. Randy is starting a fire under the box-spring grill. I look around for Allie, but she has disappeared.

A couple of minutes later she emerges from the trees. She sees me looking at her and grins.

"If you have to go, we got a sort of toilet back there," she says. "Look for the roll of TP."

"Good to know."

She starts transferring the remaining groceries into a cardboard box between the two tents. I'm wondering who sleeps where. Two tents, two guys, one girl. Does Allie have her own tent, or is she hooked up with one of them?

I go over and help her organize the groceries. Cans and bottles on one side, bagged items on the other. Allie tears open the bag of Funyuns and offers it to me. I take a handful. I've never had Funyuns before. They're oniony but not much fun.

We get the food sorted out. Allie is sitting cross-legged on the ground eating Funyuns and watching Randy work on the fire.

I'm not sure what to do. I helped them carry their stolen groceries, and now I've seen their camp. Maybe it's time for me to leave.

I say, "Well, it was nice to meet you."

"Yeah, hey, thanks for the lift, Cake," Bran says. Clearly I have served my purpose as far as he's concerned. Randy, carrying an armload of dead wood over to the fire pit, says nothing.

"You're not leaving, are you?" Allie says.

I shrug. "I should probably get going."

"Why don't you stay? Randy's going to cook something. He used to work at the Majestic."

Bran laughs and cracks open a can of beer. "Yeah, he was a dishwasher."

"Sure, but he can cook," Allie said. "Right, Randy? What are you going to make?"

"Hot dogs," Randy says. He is arranging a pyramid of sticks under the bedspring grill.

"Fine dining, just like the Majestic," Bran says.

"They're organic," Randy says.

"You helped with the groceries," Allie says to me. "You should stay for dinner at least."

In fact, I *am* hungry. I haven't eaten since the Burger King back in Pontoon Beach. A hot dog sounds good.

"Okay," I say. Bran gulps his beer and shoots me a look that makes me think it's not okay, but Allie is smiling.

"Great!" she says. She ducks into one of the tents — the smaller one — and comes out holding some plastic plates and a roll of paper towels. She brushes some leaves off the picnic table and sets out four plates. Bran is over by the fire drinking his beer and talking with Randy. Allie is telling me about the Renaissance Festival circuit.

"Have you ever been to one?" she asks.

"Once. In Minnesota. A long time ago." My parents took me. I must have been about eight. I remember trying to eat a giant turkey leg and watching a juggler. It was hot and dusty, and everybody was wearing costumes and we didn't stay long.

*That turkey leg was cooked in an electric fryer*, Dad said. *What a crock.*

"I haven't been to that one," Allie says. "The Louisiana RenFest is supposed to be great. Last one we did, the Sleepy Hollow fest up in Iowa, I was Mirabella, a serving wench." She bends over the cardboard box and finds a bottle of ketchup and a squeeze bottle of mustard. In an English accent she says, "In service of the Earl of Sandwich, royal purveyor of layered comestibles, savory tarts, strong ales, and Oscar Mayer bangers, I hereby offer rare condiments for the enjoyment of our discerning patrons." She grins at me and places the bottles on the table. "The best part is the parties after everybody leaves at the end of the day. You should come with us! I'm sure you could get a job."

"Seriously?" The idea appeals to me for a moment. Then I imagine myself wearing a costume and talking with a fake English accent. I imagine my dad seeing me like that. "I don't think I'd look good in pantaloons."

She tips her head and studies me. "With a leather tunic and knee-high boots, you'd look quite princely."

Bran crumples his empty beer can, walks over to the cooler, and grabs another.

"Do you want a beer?" Allie asks.

I don't, but I say, "Are you having one?"

She smiles and shakes her head. "Water?"

"Sure."

She goes over to the cooler and finds two bottles of water. Bran doesn't look at her. Randy has opened a package of hot dogs and is laying them out on the grill, lining them up precisely. No doubt something he learned at the Majestic while washing dishes.

"Randy doesn't say much," I observe.

"He has a rich internal life. You should've seen the sculptures he was making at KCAI—these wire-and-glass-shard things that looked like tornadoes."

"How come you quit?"

"I didn't really. Just taking a gap year."

"What kind of art did you do?"

She snorts. "Paintings that sucked." She goes back to the cardboard box, gets a bag of hot dog buns, and plunks them onto the table.

"Whole wheat," Randy says.

A few minutes later Randy declares the hot dogs to be cooked. He picks them off the grill with his fingers and arranges them artistically on a plastic plate. We all sit at the table and make a meal of hot dogs and Funyuns. Randy and Bran are drinking beer; Allie and I stick with water. The conversation flows fast— even Randy is talking, but it's all about the festival in Iowa, and people I don't know, and things that might have been funny if I'd been there. Mostly I'm watching how often Bran scowls at me, and how often Allie smiles. Randy doesn't even seem to know I'm present. I eat three hot dogs and half a bag of Funyuns while thinking about how to gracefully make my exit.

Finally the food is gone. I stand up first and start to say thank you, but Allie interrupts me.

"Stiggy, you want to help me with the dishes?"

Dishes? There are four plastic plates and that's it.

"Um . . . okay," I say.

Bran goes back to the cooler for another beer. He cracks it open and watches as I follow Allie into the woods. We soon come to a crushed-gravel walkway.

"People come here to look at birds," she says. "Mostly they stay on these trails, so nobody bothers us." We cross the trail and continue through the woods. The brush is so thick, I can only see a few yards in any direction. After a couple of minutes the trees open up and we are looking out onto the lake. Allie squats at the water's edge and cleans the plates, scrubbing them with sand, no soap. She stacks them on a driftwood log, then walks a few yards along the rocky shore and reaches into a pile of brush.

"Help me with this." She is tugging at something. I see the front end of a canoe. I grab hold, and we slide the canoe out from its hiding place.

"You hauled a canoe out here?"

"Bran found it."

"*Found* it?"

"Well . . ." Allie laughs. "Borrowed it, maybe."

We drag the canoe down to the shore and nose it onto the water. She clambers into the front. I hop in back. We grab paddles from the bottom of the canoe and push out onto the lake. The water is dead calm. We pull in our paddles and float.

"This is nice," I say.

She turns around in her seat, leans against the prow, and tips her head back. The way she moves is so loose and natural that it's almost as if she is made of liquid, as if I could touch her and my hand would sink in to the wrist.

"No clouds," she says. "Do you know what that means?"

"No rain?" The sky is deep blue above, becoming the color of a ripe peach where it touches the horizon. I wonder how the blue becomes orange without any green in between.

"It means it's going to be a chilly night," Allie says. "Do you have a sleeping bag?"

"Yeah, I do," I say. I threw one in the trunk when I was packing, just in case I decided to camp out. I'm not sure if she is asking me to stay with them, or how that would work. There are only two tents. "It's in my car," I say.

She is still looking up at the sky.

"Is Bran your boyfriend?" I ask.

"He wishes he was," she says. "I don't actually know him that well. Like I said, we just met him up in Iowa. He was on the cleanup crew. Anyway, it turned out the three of us were all going to the Louisiana fair, and we had no in-between plans."

"So, you and Randy?"

"We're just friends now."

"Oh." I try to imagine being *just friends* with Gaia. Sleeping in the next tent.

"So, you had a girlfriend back in Minnesota?"

"Not anymore."

"But you have friends?"

I think about that. I did have friends from back in middle school, but I quit hanging with them a year or so ago. My oldest friend, Jimmy McCarthy, got into smoking weed, and I didn't like getting high, or the guys he started hanging with. Fonzo Garcia hooked up with this girl Annie and pretty much spent all his time with her. Van Johnson's parents sent him to a private school in Hopkins, and he acquired a bunch of rich friends. Geoff Kinney, when we were in ninth grade, borrowed my Darth Vader TIE fighter and broke it and never said he was sorry or bought me a new one, so he was history too.

Then there was Garf Neff, my newest friend and the only guy I'd been hanging out with lately, but after the last time I saw him, I don't think he'd call himself my friend anymore.

"I don't think I have *any* friends."

"I don't believe you."

"Yeah, right, because you know everything about me." I don't mean for it to come out mean and sarcastic, but it does.

Allie is not fazed. "You have friends," she says confidently. "You just don't know how to let them *be* your friends."

"They need permission?"

Allie sits up and leans forward. The canoe rocks.

"What do you think a friend *is*?" she asks.

I think for a moment, then say, "Somebody who doesn't screw you over."

"Friends can screw you over."

"Then I'm not friends with them anymore."

She looks at me for a long time, then says, "That's kind of sad. Forgiveness is what makes friendships solid and real."

"I can forgive people. I just don't trust them after that."

"After what?"

"After screwing me over."

"What about you? Have you ever done something

to one of your friends and had them dump you just because of that one thing?"

I think about Gaia, and I think, *I must have done something*. I think about Garf.

I nod.

"Then maybe they weren't really your friend. You know what a friend is really? It's somebody you can let help you."

"You mean anybody that helps you is your friend?"

"No." Her brow furrows, and she stares at her clasped hands. Like she's thinking hard, wanting to get it right.

She says, "It's somebody you *let* help. Because it takes two, you know? The helper and the one who invites her—or him—in. Like in vampire movies. The vampire can't come into your house unless you invite him."

"The helpful vampire?" I say.

"More like Jesus," she says, completely serious.

I had a feeling this would get religious.

"Jesus was a vampire?" I ask, hoping to derail her.

"He did come back from the dead, right? But he had a lot of friends."

"Yeah, twelve. And one sold him out." I spent most of my church time ogling Cella Kimball's ponytail, but I must have learned a few things.

"Actually, three of them did—Judas, Peter, and Thomas. I mean, Peter denied knowing him three times, and Thomas didn't believe the resurrected

Jesus was real until he met him in the flesh. But Jesus forgave them, right?"

"So are you, like, really religious?"

"Not at all." She unclasps her hands. "I think the Bible has some pretty good stories, but that's all they are. Stories."

"Is Bran a friend?"

"Sure he is. But, you know, different rules for different friends."

"He doesn't like me much."

"He's a lot like you."

"Bran? No, he's not."

"You know that thing you said about a friend being somebody who doesn't screw you over? That's something Bran would say. He always expects the worst from everybody. He doesn't think he has any friends either."

# Past

**I knew I'd acted like a jerk at the park over** that bench thing, but Gaia must have forgiven me, because the next time I saw her, everything seemed cool. We did stuff. I saw her nearly every day. Neither of us had much money, so a lot of times we just sat around doing nothing—just talking, or her reading a book and me pretending to read, like old people. It was kind of boring, but I liked it.

Of course, I would have liked it better if we'd been having a lot of sex, but we weren't. We weren't having any. Except for making out, but that was hard because it just made me want more. Gaia had decided we should take it slow. Frustrating? Yes, but I figured I could wait.

She liked to talk about art. I asked her if she wanted to be an artist, but she said she didn't.

"I'm not talented," she said. "I just know what I like."

"What do you like?"

She shrugged. "I like Georgia O'Keeffe. I like Frida Kahlo."

"How come you only like women artists?"

"I like van Gogh."

"But mostly you like women."

"Well, I like you." She grinned. Gaia had a special sort of grin—chin down, eyes looking up, a dimple at the left corner of her mouth. She didn't do it often, and it always made me feel tender and confused. It took me a second to remember what we were talking about.

"I mean you like women artists," I said. "Are you a feminist?"

"Are you a masculist?"

"That isn't even a thing!"

She laughed. "Actually, I think I'd like to study art. Not to make it, but just to learn about it."

"Like your dad?"

"No, not like him." She looked away. "I don't know what I want."

Because I was spending so much time with Gaia last summer, I didn't see much of Garf. I figured he was just hanging out at Brain Food or playing Hearthstone or doing other Garf stuff without me. I didn't miss him.

I was with Gaia one time at the Main Squeeze. Gaia was standing at the counter looking at the menu. It's huge—they sell every sort of drink you can imagine, including their version of a Black Mamba, which I was definitely not ordering. I just wanted a latte. Boring, I know, but it was what I wanted. Gaia had to read every single item on the menu board before deciding.

I spotted Garf sitting at one of the tables in back with Geoff Kinney, the guy who'd busted my Darth Vader TIE fighter back in the ninth grade. That bugged me, Garf being friendly with Geoff. They made for an odd-looking pair: Garf all lanky and pointy, and Geoff doing his impression of a potato. I walked over to their table.

"Frick and Frack," I said.

It was something my dad used to say. We had a couple of neighbors, Robert and Jonathan, who were always fixing their house and borrowing Dad's tools. Half the time he'd have to go over and help them, because they didn't know what they were doing. He called them Frick and Frack, but not to their faces. I'd see him coming out of the garage with his toolbox, and he'd say, "Frick and Frack have a leaking toilet." Then he'd go help them fix it. When I was little, I thought that "Frick" and "Frack" were their real names. Later I thought maybe it meant they were gay. But then I heard him use the phrase to describe other guys who weren't gay, so I figured out it just meant they were incompetent.

Garf looked up and said, "Huh?" Like he'd never heard of Frick and Frack, and maybe he hadn't. He was drinking bubble tea. Geoff was sucking on something that had a four-inch cap of whipped cream on top.

"Frick and Frack," I repeated. "You guys on a date?"

Geoff thought that was hilarious; Garf took it literally, as Garf would do.

"No. Geoff was just telling me a trick for winning at Hearthstone," Garf said.

Hearthstone is an online game Garf and I played once. I was no good at it, so I quit, but Garf liked it.

"You got to use the mill rogue deck," Geoff said. "Get 'em drawing cards, that's the secret!"

I wasn't completely sure what a "mill rogue deck" was, and I really didn't care.

"Wow. That's *so* amazing," I said in my most unamazed voice.

Geoff continued, oblivious. "They got a full hand, but they keep drawing anyway, and every time they do, one of their other cards is destroyed, but by the time they realize what's happening, *bam*! They're out of draws and you got 'em. Works every time. Try it!"

"Yeah, next time I decide to dork out, I'll for sure give it a try."

Geoff didn't blink. For him "dork" was probably a compliment, but Garf was giving me this hurt look. I didn't care.

"You ever gonna replace my TIE fighter?" I said to Geoff.

He blinked that time, and sat back. "That was two years ago!" he said, his cheeks turning pink. "Besides, it was broke when you borrowed it to me."

"I didn't *borrow* it to you. I *lent* it to you," I said, channeling my dad, the grammar cop. "And it was in *perfect* condition."

Geoff giggled. Maybe it was just a nervous giggle, but it got to me.

"Why are you hanging out with this fat asshole?" I asked Garf.

Garf stared at me as if he'd never seen me before. Geoff's whole face was red. I really wanted to grab his whipped cream drink and pour it over his head, but a little voice inside reminded me that Gaia was probably watching, and I'd already gotten us kicked out of Wigglesworth's.

"You guys deserve each other," I said.

Garf winced as if I'd slapped him, and for a moment I felt bad. I turned my back on them and walked over to the counter. Gaia was talking to the counter guy. She hadn't been watching at all. *I should've tipped that drink in his lap*, I thought. At the same time I was a little proud of myself that I hadn't.

"What are you getting?" I asked Gaia. My voice sounded weird.

She frowned at me. "Are you okay?"

"I'm fine."

"You look mad."

"It's that guy sitting with Garf. I don't like him."

She looked over at them. "Geoff Kinney? Why don't you like him?"

I was not about to tell her the whole stupid ancient TIE fighter story.

"Never mind," I said. "Look, can we just go?"

"I haven't ordered."

"Let's go to the Starbucks."

"Why?"

I couldn't make any words come out.

"God, look at you. Are you sure you're okay?"

I wasn't okay. I was angry and I was embarrassed.

She took my hand, and we walked out of the Squeeze, across the street to the little postage-stamp-size park, and sat down on the bench by a statue of some guy on a horse.

"Talk," she said.

"He just really bugs me," I said. "That chunked-out moron sitting there with Garf."

"Why?" she asked.

"I don't know."

"Are you jealous because you're not Garf's only friend?"

"Yeah, right, like I care who Garf's friends are."

She laughed. I laughed too, but I don't think either of us thought anything was funny.

"You should call him. Go hang out at the comic shop or whatever it is you guys used to do."

"I thought you didn't like Garf."

"I don't like or dislike him. I hardly know him. I just . . . what I said before, I just didn't like him having us—you know—on replay in his brain."

I imagined us, on my bed, living in Garf's brain.

"But I'd say that about anybody," she said.

# "One of These Days"

## Pink Floyd
## 5:58

**It's getting dark. Allie and I paddle back to** shore and hide the canoe in the brush. On the way back Allie clasps my hand. Her palm is warm and moist. She holds on as we follow the path, but lets go as soon as we reach the camp. Randy and Bran are sitting by the fire drinking beer. Bran is smoking a cigarette. Randy looks sleepy, but Bran's eyes flash in the firelight; I can feel them stabbing at me. He flicks his cigarette into the fire, sending up a spray of glowing ashes.

"You guys have a nice time?" he says in a splintery voice.

Allie smiles. I'm coming to realize that her smiles do not mean she's happy. I can tell she's uncomfortable.

"Cut it out, Bran."

He snorts. "The queen of the camp speaks." He elbows Randy. Randy doesn't react. Bran goes back to the cooler for another beer.

"You should go get your sleeping bag," Allie says to me quietly. "Don't worry about Bran. It's just how he is."

"Okay." I'm glad to be leaving at that moment, and not entirely sure I'll be coming back.

"Don't get lost!" Bran calls after me. "There's bears out there!"

I don't think there are bears, but I am a little worried about finding my way back to the parking lot. It's almost completely dark. I follow the trail through the woods and out into the open area. I can see the causeway, and lights on the far side of the lake. It only takes me ten minutes to get to the parking lot. There are no other cars. I open the trunk and take out the tightly rolled sleeping bag that I haven't used since Dad took me camping when I was twelve. I hope I still fit.

I balance the bag on the spoiler and get in the car behind the wheel and try to think. Am I crazy to camp out with them? Allie is nice. Randy is practically inert. Bran makes me nervous.

I turn on the stereo and scroll through the iPod looking for some big beats and find an old song by Pink Floyd, mostly just wind sounds and a heavy bass line—with the volume up and the subwoofer booming, it's like a thunderstorm happening inside my chest.

Maybe I'd be best off just driving away. Find another cheap hotel, or sleep in the car. On the other hand, I'm really tired, and even though Bran is a jerk, I don't think he's dangerous. It's not as if they're shooting heroin or sacrificing babies or anything like that—they're just college dropouts working Renaissance Festivals and trying to get by.

And then there's Allie, with her red hair and freckles and her liquid body and that smile. So different from Gaia. Allie doesn't seem quite real. Gaia was totally real. Allie is more like an idea than a real person. In a way that makes her even more attractive, more sexy, like an actress in a movie, or a model on the pages of a magazine. The thought of touching her tingles my entire body, and I'm pretty sure that if I go back, I'll be touching her.

I make a decision. Maybe it's my body that makes the decision. I shove the iPod and the earbuds in my pocket, get out, lock the car, grab my sleeping bag, and walk back over the causeway. I cross the open area, and I'm looking for the path into the woods when a figure emerges from the trees.

"Dude! Hey, dude!" It's Bran. He looks bigger because he's wearing his backpack.

"Hi," I say, a little nervous.

"Thought maybe you'd gotten lost." He seems friendly enough. A little drunk, though.

"I had to fight off some bears," I say.

He laughs. "Look, I just want to say, Allie really

likes you, y'know? And it's cool. She's cute, and I think she wants to do you. I know I was kind of unfriendly before, but that's just me being an asshole. I'm sorry. "

I'm startled by that. Assholes rarely admit to their own assholery.

"That's okay," I say.

"Listen, I left a carton of cigs in your car."

"You were smoking at camp," I say.

"Yeah, I ran out. I'm having a nic fit. Is your car locked?"

"Yeah, of course it is." I turn back toward the causeway. "Okay, let's go get your cigs."

"Whoa, hey, you don't have to walk all the way back there. Just give me your keys, and I'll go."

I hesitate.

"What, you think I'm gonna steal your car? Dude! We're camp buddies. Anyways, I don't even have a license. Besides, I've had, like, six beers. I mean, come on!"

I don't really want to walk all the way back to the parking lot.

"Besides, Allie is expecting you. She was in her tent moving things around, making room. She has the hots for you."

I hand him the car keys.

"Thanks, dude." He grins, but in the dark it looks more like a snarl, white teeth set in a dark face framed by oily strands of even darker hair. "See you in a few."

He heads back toward the causeway. As his form

fades into the dark, it occurs to me to wonder why he's wearing his backpack.

When I get back to camp, Allie and Randy are sitting by the fire talking in low voices. Randy's arm is wrapped around Allie's shoulders.

"Hey," I say.

Allie looks up and smiles. I think she smiles more than anybody else I've ever known.

"You found your way back!" She frowns. "Did you run into Bran?"

"Yeah."

"Was he . . . was he acting okay?"

"He seemed fine. He said he had to get something out of my car."

Allie and Randy look at each other.

"He said he'd be right back," I say.

"We asked him to leave," Allie says. Randy looks at her. "I mean, *Randy* asked him to leave."

"Oh! Why?"

"He was acting a little weird," she says.

"Weird how?"

"Well, he was drunk, and getting kind of aggressive."

Randy emits a little snort. I think it's a laugh.

"Unpermitted touching," he says. "That's the definition of assault. My dad's a lawyer."

I am confused. "He touched *you*?" I ask Randy.

Randy gives his head a tiny shake and looks at Allie, who seems vastly uncomfortable.

"He came in my tent."

"What did he do?" I'm clenching my fists, and my face feels hot.

"Nothing. I mean, Randy grabbed him and pulled him off me before anything happened."

I'm flashing back to the mushroom caves, and for a split second Gaia and Allie become one person.

"I never liked him," Randy says.

I see Ben Gingrass's face, lit by candlelight. I see Bran's wolfish smile. Both times I was useless. My fists are clenched so hard, I can feel it all the way up my arms.

"When he gets back," I say, "I'm going to—"

"He won't be back," Randy says.

Nobody speaks for a couple of seconds. Then Allie says, "You didn't give him your keys, did you?"

I run through the woods, driven by fear and fury, then out into the open and across the field to the causeway.

I can see the parking lot. The empty parking lot.

I keep running until I skid to a stop where my car was parked. Gasping for breath, I look around. Maybe this is the wrong parking lot.

It's not.

Maybe Bran just moved the car, as a joke. *Maybe he'll bring it back*, I think.

I recall the last time I saw his face, grinning and saying, *Thanks, dude.*

He won't bring it back. I stand there, paralyzed, not knowing what to do. Call the police? I have no phone, and even if I did, what then? What could I tell them? That a guy named Bran stole my car? Except it's not technically my car? That I don't even know the license plate number? That I'm seventeen years old? From Minnesota? Staying in an illegal camp on an island with a couple of art school dropouts?

I don't think so.

I force myself to breathe normally and take stock. I still have money in my wallet. I have the iPod. I have the clothes I'm wearing.

I have a place to stay the night.

The fire has burned down to embers by the time I find my way back to the camp. I don't see Allie or Randy, but the faint glow of a candle is coming through the wall of the bigger tent.

"Hello?" I say.

I hear some scuffling. The flap opens, and Allie sticks her head out. Her hair is even wilder than usual; I can barely see her face.

"You're back," she says.

"Where would I go? Bran stole my car."

She nods, unsurprised, then ducks back inside. More scuffling about, and soft voices. Allie crawls out of the tent holding a small flashlight. She is barefoot, wearing gym shorts and a sleeveless tee.

"Are you okay?" she asks.

"Not really. Do you think there's any chance he'll bring it back?"

"I doubt it. He'll probably just drive it to wherever he's going and leave it there. Kansas City, maybe. That's where he's from. You'll probably get it back eventually."

I don't say anything. Kansas City is three hundred miles away, on the other side of Missouri. Even if I went there, what could I do? Technically, I stole the car too.

"You shouldn't have given him the keys," she says.

"You *think*?"

"Sorry," she says quickly. "I guess that was kind of obvious."

"It's not your fault."

"I should have warned you about him."

I shrug.

"I cleared out my tent for you. I left a candle and matches in there. Maybe we can figure something out in the morning."

Even though the answer is clear, I have to ask. "Where are you sleeping?"

With her flashlight she gestures toward the bigger tent. I nod, push my sleeping bag through the flap of the small tent, and crawl in after it.

# X-Men

**When I think back over last summer, I think** of breathing. Long, slow inhalations. Breathe in, Gaia fills my world. Those were the times we grew close, almost as if we became one creature. Exhale, and those were the bad times when she would withdraw, or I would say something stupid and she'd get mad. Then the in-between times, groping in the dark, trying to find each other. How many cycles did we go through? Why did it keep happening?

The day after I had the run-in with Geoff Kinney at the Squeeze, I called Garf. I had a whole speech ready to leave on his voice mail, but he picked up on the third ring.

"Hey," he said.

"Hey."

I waited for him to say something, but he didn't. So I launched into my prepared remarks.

"Listen, I'm sorry I acted like a jerk. I was having a bad day."

That was pretty much my whole speech.

He waited, I guess to make sure that was all, then said, "Okay."

"So, we cool?"

"You kind of freaked out Geoff, you know."

"Yeah, well, he wrecked my TIE fighter."

"Yeah, and you wrecked my mint copy of X-Men number twenty-five. The one where Wolverine loses his Adamantium!"

It was true. I had spilled Coke on it.

"That was an accident."

"Yeah, and I didn't give you grief about it."

"You want me to buy you a new one?"

"It was worth, like, forty bucks."

I winced. "Seriously?"

"It used to be. Before you spilled Coke on it. Anyway, you should cut Geoff some slack."

"Okay. But I still don't like him."

"You don't like anybody."

"That's what Gaia says, but it's not true. I like her. And you're not so bad."

"Thanks a lot. How about the other seven and a half billion people on the planet?"

"I haven't met them all."

# "Back to Black"

## Amy Winehouse
## 4:00

**That night in the little tent was the longest** night ever. Tossing, turning, fantasizing about catching Bran, punching him in the face, getting my car back. . . . The sleeping bag too hot. I unzip it and doze off and wake up shivering. And the rain. Thunder at first, then lightning bright enough to light up the walls of the tent. A patter of fat raindrops followed by a deluge. Water leaking in through the flap, through the seams. Water everywhere.

I must have slept a little. I open my eyes, and one wall of the tent is lit up by the sun. I never undressed last night except for taking off my shoes and socks. The backs of my jeans and shirt are soaked. I wriggle out of my sodden sleeping bag and crawl outside. It's *cold*. The sky is bright blue and cloudless. The wet grass is sagging from the rain. If it was any colder, the grass would be frosted.

Allie and Randy are trying to get the fire started. Allie is tearing pages out of a paperback book, one at a time, crumpling them. Randy adds the pages to a small pyramid of smoldering sticks.

Allie looks up at me and smiles. A giant asteroid could be heading for Earth; she'd look up at it and smile.

"Did your tent leak?" she asks.

I nod.

"Ours too," she says. With a smile.

Randy ducks his head down sideways and blows on the paper and twigs; a small flame appears.

"More pages," he says.

Allie looks at the book in her hands. "But we're getting to the part I haven't read yet!"

"Tear off the cover," he says. She does so; he feeds it to the growing flames.

"I never thought of myself as a book burner," she says.

I stand barefoot on the cold wet grass and watch them. Randy keeps feeding the fire little sticks that hiss as they touch the flame, then darken, smoke, and catch. He adds a chunk of driftwood and watches hopefully as the small fire dries the surface. I feel as if I should help, so I go over to the cardboard box where Allie stored some of the groceries. There is one bag of Funyuns left. I toss it to Randy.

"Funyuns for breakfast?" he says.

"For the fire. They burn great."

He frowns at the bag, shrugs, and stuffs it under the driftwood. The bag bursts into flames. Randy quickly piles on more sticks and branches, and soon we have a real fire. I move in close, sucking up the heat.

"Cold wave coming," Randy says. "Time to head south."

We warm our hands at the fire. Eventually it burns down to a bed of glowing embers, and Randy puts the bedspring grill over it. Allie digs in the cooler and comes up with a box of strawberry Pop-Tarts. She lays all twelve of them on the grill, lining them up neatly, like cards in a game of solitaire. We all stare at the Pop-Tarts as they cook, hypnotized by the colored sprinkles on white frosting. As soon the edges turn dark brown, Allie lifts them off the grill and piles them on a red plastic plate.

I'm not that hungry, but I crave warmth. I eat four of them. Allie eats three. Randy eats the rest. Nobody is talking. I crawl back inside the tent for my shoes and socks. They didn't get wet. It feels glorious to pull dry socks over my cold damp feet. I pull out the wet sleeping bag and drape it over the tent to dry.

"What are you going to do?" Allie asks me.

Last night she was trying to talk me into going to Louisiana with them, but this morning I hear no invitation in her voice, and her smile means nothing.

"I'm going back to the parking lot to see if Bran returned my car."

Randy snorts out a laugh. "He's probably back in Kansas City by now."

"I'm going to check anyways," I say.

By the time the parking lot is in sight, my feet are soaked from walking through the wet grasses. There is no Mustang. No anything. I head back to the camp. When I get there, Allie and Randy are rolling up the bigger tent.

"You're going today?" I ask, although it's obvious.

Allie smiles. I'm starting to find her smile really irritating.

"No car?" she guesses.

I shake my head and watch them struggling with the wet nylon.

"How are you going to get there?" I ask.

Allie smiles, and this time it is definitely forced. "We were hoping you could, you know, drive us down, but now . . ."

"We'll hitch," Randy says. He pulls the straps tight on the tightly rolled tent.

"You think I could get a job at the festival?" I ask, even though I'm pretty sure by now that their plans included me only as long as I had a car.

"Maybe," Allie says slowly.

Randy says, "We're hitching. Nobody's going to stop for all three of us."

*Okay, that seems pretty clear.*

"There's no guarantee of a job once you get there," Allie says, barely holding on to her smile.

"Last night you said there were lots of jobs."

Finally her smile goes away completely. I feel a sick sense of triumph.

"Maybe you could be the guy with his head and hands in the stocks," Randy says with an unpleasant laugh. "People could throw tomatoes at you. You'd be perfect."

"If you have money, you could take a bus," Allie says.

"You have money?" Randy suddenly looks very interested in me.

"No," I say, but I say it too quickly. They can tell I'm lying. "Not much," I say.

"How much?" Randy asks. I have nothing but my wet clothes and a soggy wallet, and my iPod.

"I'm leaving," I say, and start walking.

"Don't you want your sleeping bag?" Allie calls after me.

I don't want to haul around a soaking wet sleeping bag. I keep going. I'm at the causeway when I hear a shout. I look back. Allie is running across the field toward me.

"Stiggy, wait!" She is carrying something dark under her arm. Does she want to come with me? Did Randy do something? All these thoughts flick through my brain in seconds, even though I'm not sure I want any of them to be true.

Allie stops and thrusts the thing she is carrying at me. It's a sweatshirt. A zippered, dark blue hoodie.

"Take this," she says, breathing heavily. "It was Bran's."

"I don't want anything of his."

"It's cold." Allie is trying to smile but is not quite getting there. "You'll freeze."

It *is* cold. I take the hoodie. There is a white arrow-head shape on the chest with the initials KC in red. On the back is the word "CHIEFS."

"Bran's a football fan?"

"Look, I'm sorry," she says. "I really thought it would be cool if we could all go to the RenFest together, but—"

"But Randy doesn't want me around."

"It would be . . . awkward."

I put on the hoodie. It's dry, and it fits.

"Are you going to be okay? I mean, are you going back to Minnesota?"

"I haven't decided."

"I'm really sorry."

"I wasn't going with you anyway."

"Oh." She takes a step back and half smiles. "Okay."

I turn my back to her and walk off across the cause-way with no idea where I'm going. Just like I thought I wanted.

# On the Beach

**All the way through the rest of July and most** of August I saw Gaia every day. We did things. Even if sometimes—like that day when we walked to East River Park—they didn't turn out so good. Even when I acted like a jerk, or when she was mopey and withdrawn, we still needed to be together. I felt empty when she wasn't around.

During those weeks I always had a Trojan with me. I have it now as I stand in the empty parking lot and stare at the space where my car used to be, and wonder what to do next. Where to go.

With Gaia I was always hoping we'd end up someplace private, someplace we could melt into each other and, well, have sex again. But it didn't happen. Only

that once. I asked her about it a couple of times—
okay, a lot of times—but she always slid the conversation around to something else. It was frustrating.
She was happy to kiss, to press her body to mine, but
when I tried for more, she would push my hands away.

"Not now," she would say. I bet she said it a hundred times.

"Why?" I'd ask her. "When?"

"I want to," she would say. Then she'd kiss me and
we'd hold each other, and then she'd push me away.
"Just not right now." She would grab my hand, and
we'd keep walking or doing whatever it was we'd
been doing.

One hot August day at the swimming beach on the
Saint Croix—boats on the river, families all around
us, kids splashing in the shallows—I asked her again.

"So how come we did it that one time?"

She didn't answer right away.

A mom and dad with two boys—one a toddler, the
other maybe five years old—were sitting near us on a
big beach blanket. The mom was spreading sunscreen
onto the older boy's back. A couple of stoners rubber-
legged their way past us and waded into the water.
One of them, a pot-bellied guy with long blond hair,
stopped knee deep and said, "Whoa!" The smile on
his face was flabby and loose; the whites of his wide-
open eyes glowed red. "My toes are going, like, *whoa*!"
His friend joined him, and they stood there wriggling
their toes in the river sand and going, "Whoa."

"Because I wanted it to be my decision," Gaia said.

"Huh?" I'd been watching the stoners, and it took me a second to remember the question I'd asked her.

"It really scared me, what almost happened," she said.

"What do you mean? You mean because you could've gotten pregnant?"

"No!" She gave me that incredulous *Are you even listening?* look. "I mean, what almost happened in the *caves!*"

"You mean with Ben?"

"Yes! What if he'd done it? What if the first time I had sex, it was rape?" She dragged her forefinger through the sand next to the blanket, making a spiral. "Would that make sex bad for the rest of my life?"

"Uh . . . *was* it?"

"No!" She looked at me and smiled. "I'm glad we did it. You were sweet."

"I am not sweet."

"You are when you want to be." She looked over at the family with the kids. The father was helping the older boy build a lumpy sandcastle. "You could be a good dad."

"I don't want to be *any* kind of dad," I say.

"Me neither. I mean, be a mom. At least I don't think so."

The stoners moved off, wading along the shore, still going, "Whoa."

"So why don't we do it anymore? I got condoms."

"So you've mentioned. About a hundred times."

I thought about my wallet, and how if you looked at the back of it, you could see a faint circle pressed into the leather. The shape of a rolled-up Trojan, still in its wrapping.

"We don't have to if you don't want to," I said.

Her face went hard. "What do you mean?"

"I mean, it's okay."

"Are you sure that's what you mean?" She had that angry edge in her voice, and I couldn't figure out why.

"What did I say?"

Gaia compressed her lips and looked out across the water and shook her head.

"Nothing. I don't know."

"Yes, you do."

She took a breath and said, "Okay. It sounded like you were promising not to *force* me."

"I was? I didn't . . . *What*?"

"You said I didn't have to if I didn't want to. That should go without saying."

I thought about that for a moment.

"That wasn't what I meant," I said.

"I know that. It's the kind of thing guys say all the time, and they don't think they mean it. Like it's their decision to make."

"I just meant . . ." What *had* I meant?

I'm still not sure.

I think about Bran, drunk, crawling into the tent

after Allie, and what would have happened if Randy hadn't stopped him. And how Randy made Bran leave, and how that led to Bran stealing my car, and now Allie was sleeping with Randy, who she'd told me she'd broken up with. . . . Was that the same thing? Would Allie know what Gaia had been talking about? I think about the stripper at that café, whose job it was to make men want her body. Would she know? I think about Garf's sort-of-cousin Kelsey, who, according to Garf, "sort of seduced" him. Was that really what happened?

Anyway, I keep thinking about that day at the beach.

# "River Deep— Mountain High"
## Ike and Tina Turner
### 3:37

**I am walking because I don't know what** else to do. I follow the road along the lakeshore, listening to the iPod. The wind coming off the water feels like tiny knives. I jam my fists in the pockets of the hoodie. There's a crumpled piece of paper in the right-hand pocket. I take it out and almost toss it, but then I think what my dad would say about me littering, so I stuff it back in the pocket. I'll wait until I see a trash can.

I turn north into a residential area. It looks kind of like Gaia's neighborhood—lots of ramblers and double garages. I keep going, one foot in front of the other. At least if I keep walking, I'll stay warm. Eventually my jeans and shoes will dry.

Maybe Bran didn't go to Kansas City. Maybe I'll find

the Mustang parked by the side of the road. Maybe he left the keys in it.

A woman with a big, crazy voice is singing about love. I know that voice, but I can't think who it is, so I check the iPod display. Tina Turner. She was in a movie I saw once.

Maybe I'll look up and find Gaia standing in front of me. It's not impossible. I construct an elaborate fantasy in which she has concealed a GPS tracker in the Mustang and tracked it down. I find her sitting in the passenger seat waiting for me.

The damp jeans are chafing my crotch. I stop and try to adjust them. I'm on a sort of highway, a four-lane road with lots of businesses. I just passed a QuikTrip, a school, and a shopping mall. How long have I been walking? I have no idea where I am. The sun is high, and it's warmer now. I unzip the hoodie and look around. Ahead on the right I spot a Burger King sign. The same BK I ate lunch at . . . was it just yesterday?

My stomach pulls me forward, and a few minutes later I'm sitting in a back booth with a Whopper, large fries, and a thirty-eight-ounce Coca-Cola. I wolf down the burger and drink half of the Coke, then slow down and pick at the fries while I sort through my options.

I've already figured out that reporting the Mustang stolen will only make things worse. Maybe the cops will find it sometime, and see that it's registered to my father, and maybe Mom will be notified. I'm really not sure how that works. Or they might find it and stick it in an impound lot and never tell anybody. I could call my mom and tell her what happened, and she could report it. But that would mean calling my mom.

I have her credit card. It still works—I used it to pay for the food. So she must be seeing these charges on her account. She knows how to access that stuff online. She must know I'm alive, and roughly where I am. I could use it to buy a bus ticket—or even a plane ticket—home. That's probably what she'd want me to do. Do I want to go home? I think about what's waiting for me, and except for one very pissed-off mom, I got nothing.

I take out my wallet and count my remaining cash. Three hundred and six dollars. What did I spend a hundred bucks on? Food, sodas, a John Deere cap—it adds up.

The fries are gone, and I haven't figured out one single thing. I watch a guy in a Burger King shirt wiping tables. Maybe I could get a job doing that. I think I could handle it. He gets to my table and points at my tray.

"Want me to take that for you?"

"Sure." He lifts the tray and its contents with one hand and wipes down the table with his rag. Pretty fancy service for a Burger King. As he carries my tray and trash away, I remember the crumpled paper in my pocket. I dig it out, and I'm about to walk it over to the trash can when, out of curiosity,

I flatten the paper to see what it is. It's a cell phone bill. Three pages. Dated last July. $240.16, including the unpaid balance from May. The name on the bill is Brandon T. Fetzig. The address on the bill is in Prairie Village, Kansas.

# Closed Mondays

**Most of Gaia's black T-shirts had paintings by** artists I'd never heard of, like this one that was printed with a bunch of pinkish shapes that looked like body parts, but I couldn't make out what was what.

"What's that on your shirt?" I asked.

She looked down. "It's a painting."

"Did you paint it?"

"It's a Lee Krasner painting."

"I never heard of him."

"It's a *her*. She was married to Jackson Pollock. My dad gave it to me."

Another time she had one with this wavy black-and-white-striped image that made my eyes all jiggly. She told me it was a painting by Bridget Riley. Later

I looked up Bridget Riley online. She made all these wild op-art things. I noticed that one of her paintings was at the Walker Art Center in Minneapolis, so the next day I suggested to Gaia that we go there.

"I didn't think you were interested in stuff like that." She sounded surprised.

"I liked the shirt you wore yesterday. They say on their website that they have a Bridget Riley painting. Also, it's supposed to rain, and the museum is indoors, and it's free."

"Oh. Have you ever been there?"

"No, but I know where it is."

"Okay, sure. How are we going to get there?"

That was a problem. My mom was still mad at me for taking Dad's car, and Gaia didn't have her license, so getting to the Walker would require taking a bus. I'd never liked buses. I didn't even like taking the bus to school, and that was only about a ten-minute ride. But we figured out which bus to get on, and what bus to transfer to, and it wasn't that bad except for this one smelly guy sitting in front of us.

By the time we got to the Walker, it was raining. We ran down the sidewalk and up the steps to the glass doors.

"Uh-oh," Gaia said.

"What?"

She pointed at the sign on the glass.

CLOSED MONDAYS.

"Is it Monday?" I asked, stupidly.

"It is definitely Monday."

So much for my great idea of going to look at art. We stood in the shelter of the entryway and looked out at the wet world. It wasn't pouring, just a steady, warm drizzle that made everything look soft and shiny.

"We could walk through the sculpture garden." Gaia pointed across the street. "I mean, since we came all this way."

"Okay," I said. I was so embarrassed, I'd have agreed to anything. "If you don't mind getting wet."

"We'll have it all to ourselves. Nobody looks at art in the rain."

We crossed the street to the sculpture garden, an open area the size of several football fields. There were dozens of sculptures, many of them enormous, and no people in sight. Right in the middle was a fifty-foot-long bent spoon holding a gigantic bright red cherry. Water was squirting out of the cherry's stem. We walked up to it as close as we could get. The handle of the spoon was arched over a small pond; its bowl rested on a tiny round island.

"That's Maeve's favorite," Gaia said.

"You came here with Maeve?"

"We used to come here a lot."

I thought I had suggested something fresh and new for us to do together, but for Gaia this was just a rerun.

"One time we climbed the spoon handle." Her eyes looked bright as she remembered. "We got halfway, and the water was spraying on us, and we were laughing so hard that Maeve slipped. She grabbed my hand, and we both fell off and landed in the water. God, we got in *so* much trouble!" Gaia was grinning all across her face, and all I could think was that I'd never seen her smile like that. "My dad was *so* mad!"

"When was that?" I asked, even though I didn't really care. I kept thinking that I'd never seen Gaia laugh the way she remembered laughing with Maeve. I mean, we laughed, the two of us, but not like that. Not like we could fall off a spoon bridge because we were laughing so hard.

"Eighth grade," Gaia said. Her smile shrank down to nothing. "I miss her."

"Yeah, me too," I said.

Gaia shot me a look.

"I mean, I'm sorry she's gone," I said quickly.

"No, you're not." She turned away. I followed her along the walkway, trying to figure out what I'd said. I mean, I *knew* what I'd said. I just didn't know how bad I'd screwed up. It turned out we were okay, though. Gaia led me over to the coolest thing in the whole sculpture park: a giant, bright blue rooster on top of a light-gray, flat-topped metal pyramid. The rooster itself was the size of an elephant, and it was the bluest thing I'd ever seen. We looked at it for a while, and we were both smiling.

"I don't know if it's funny or awesome," I said.

"It's both," Gaia said. "That's what makes it so great."

"Hey, if I climb up there and get on top of the rooster, will you take a picture?"

"You can't get up there," she said.

"Yes, I can." The base was steep, and about ten feet high, but I figured if I took a run at it, I could make it to the top.

"Don't be so juvenile," she said. "We're not in eighth grade."

So much for creating a new sculpture park memory.

The next thing we looked at was a bronze of an eight-foot-long rabbit jumping over a giant bell. Gaia didn't like that one, so I pretended not to like it too.

The drizzle was getting heavier, so we headed for a glass-roofed pavilion that was sort of a sculpture all on its own, but before we got there, Gaia stopped in front of a life-size statue of a naked woman stepping out of the ripped-open belly of a wolf. I couldn't tell if the woman was supposed to have killed the wolf and had just decided to stand inside its corpse, or if she'd burst out of it like the creature in that movie *Alien*. Gaia stood looking at it for a long time. I wanted to get out of the rain—it was coming down harder—but Gaia wasn't moving.

"This could be me," she said.

"Come on," I said. "We're getting soaked."

Reluctantly she turned away. We ran to the pavilion. We got there just as the clouds got serious. The rain pounding on the glass above us was *loud*, and we could barely see across the garden. The giant chicken was fifty yards away, but all I could see was a blue chicken-shaped smudge.

I caught a whiff of something burning and looked around. We weren't alone. A man wearing a hat and a raincoat was standing at the other side of the pavilion smoking a cigar and looking out at the rain.

"Frederick!" Gaia called out, startling me.

The man's head jerked around. Gaia was walking toward him.

The man said, "Why, Ms. Nygren, fancy meeting you here!"

I followed her over to him. Up close I could see that he was older than I'd thought. He had a gray, pointy chin beard, slightly yellowed teeth, and wrinkles all around his eyes. His cigar was long and pencil-thin.

"An inclement day for outdoor art appreciation," he said.

I didn't think that was particularly funny, but Gaia laughed.

His eyes went to me, then back to Gaia.

"This is my friend Stiggy," Gaia said. "Stiggy, this is Frederick."

Frederick put his cigar in his mouth and held out his right hand. He locked his eyes on mine as we shook hands, then let go and returned his attention to Gaia.

"Art date?" he asked.

Gaia smiled—was she blushing?

"Art dates are the best," Frederick said, and laughed. "Gives you something to gawk at besides each other."

He puffed on his cigar and smiled as he let the smoke trickle out.

"We were going to see the Bridget Riley painting," I said, wanting to sound knowledgeable. "But I forgot it was Monday," I added, which made me look stupid.

"An easy mistake to make. So many days in a week. I conflate them frequently."

I thought he might be making fun of me, but I wasn't sure because I didn't know what "conflate" meant.

"Frederick is a sculptor," Gaia said.

"That's right. I come here to scope out the competition." He chuckled.

"I like the blue chicken," I say.

"Many people do. I imagine the *Spoonbridge and Cherry* is your second favorite. Grotesquely bright colors are quite popular with the public."

*Definitely* making fun. When I didn't say anything, he turned back to Gaia.

"Gaia, dear, how is your father?"

"He's good."

"Excellent! Give him my regards, will you?"

"Of course."

"Very nice to see you." He waved his cigar in a figure eight, like a priest giving a benediction. "Please proceed with your art date." He bowed slightly, tugged down the brim of his hat, and strolled out of the pavilion into the rain.

"Who was that?" I asked.

"Frederick Baldwin," she said. "He teaches at the U."

"Where your dad teaches?"

"A different department."

"Oh." I wasn't sure what that meant. "He's kind of sarcastic."

Gaia's eyebrows came together. "Why would you say that?"

"Just the way he talked."

"I think he's nice. I've known him forever. He's a friend of my dad's."

I hated that she had so much history. I hated that anything mattered to her except me.

# "Cactus"

## Pixies
## 2:17

**Prairie Village is a suburb of Kansas City.**
That's almost three hundred miles away.

I've never hitchhiked before. All I know is you
stick your thumb out, and sooner or later somebody pulls over and you hope they're not a robber
or a murderer. I stand on the entrance ramp to I-270
westbound and watch about a million cars blow
past me without slowing down. Finally one of them
pulls over.

The car looks normal enough—a boxy Ford Flex,
a family car. The guy driving looks normal too: a
paunchy, middle-aged salesman type with graying
hair and wire-rimmed eyeglasses. I climb in, and he
pulls off the edge of the entrance ramp and accelerates

onto the freeway. Country western music is playing on the radio.

"Where are you headed?" he asks.

"Kansas City," I say.

"*Goin' to Kansas City,*" he sings, then laughs. I don't get it. He says, "I'm only going halfway. I can get you to Columbia."

"Cool. Thanks." I'm not sure where Columbia is.

"Do you like music?"

"Um . . . yeah?"

"I've got satellite." He gestures at the stereo. "Anything you want. Ninety-nine stations. You like polka, there's a polka station. Sixties rock, eighties rock, show tunes, gospel, rap, you name it."

The guy on the radio is singing about his dog.

"This is fine," I say.

"So you like country?"

"Whatever you like is fine with me," I say.

"Are you in school?"

"No."

"I like your cap. Grew up on a farm. The old man loved his John Deere. You ever drive a tractor?"

I think about my dad on his forklift.

"No," I say.

"I got three kids. My oldest is about your age. How old are you?"

"Eighteen," I say, giving myself an extra year.

"Robbie's seventeen. Smart as a whip. Just started his senior year."

I don't say anything.

"Wouldn't want him hitchhiking, I'll tell you that. Not these days. Too many crazies." He's tapping his thumbs on the steering wheel in time to the music.

"I suppose," I say.

"Do you use drugs?"

"No."

"A lot of drugs out there. So what's in Kansas City? You got a girl there?"

"No. Just visiting a . . . friend."

"Robbie has a girlfriend. Beautiful girl. Cheerleader. You into sports?"

"Not really."

"Robbie's on the basketball team. Only six-three, but he's the best player on the team. Lettered when he was a sophomore. You know what those letter jackets cost? Arm and a leg. Arm and a leg, but he's a great kid so it's worth it. He's going to Dartmouth next year, already accepted, with a scholarship to boot. Ivy League. You going to college?"

It's going to be a long ride to Columbia.

# Boots

**By mid-August, Gaia and I had fallen into** a routine. I'd text her when I woke up and suggest something we could do. She'd text me back, either saying okay or suggesting something different.

My mom had recovered from me taking Dad's car back in July, so she let me use her Toyota now and then, which made things easier. Sometimes Gaia and I would just drive around listening to music. She didn't like hip-hop, but we both liked older alt-rock like the White Stripes. She liked Florence and the Machine. And Regina Spektor. And Johnette Napolitano. I'd never heard of most of them. She liked girl singers. She was sort of sexist that way, like with her art shirts. I guess the word isn't really "sexist," but I didn't know what else to call it.

Anyway, some of our best days were spent driving around listening to music, syncing our phones to the crappy stereo in Mom's Toyota. Sometimes we'd talk about the bands we both liked, but more often about the ones we agreed to hate: Coldplay, U2, the Lemonheads, Beck, the Beatles. . . . Our list of hateable bands was long, and it didn't make a lot of sense because I didn't mind some of them, but it was more about what we could agree on. It felt as if we were the only ones in the world who knew what sucked.

I used to argue with Garf about music all the time. He was mostly into dubstep and reggae, which he claimed were related, and for some reason I could never figure out, he loved Captain Beefheart.

There were a lot of things Gaia and I didn't talk about much. Like the future. One time we were sitting on the stone benches in her backyard. She was texting back and forth with Maeve, and I was just sitting there.

"Maeve has decided to go into politics," she announced.

"She wants to run for class president?"

"No, she wants to study political science and run for Congress. But first she has to get through high school." She laughed. "A month ago she wanted to be a marine biologist."

"Are you going to go to college?"

"That's not for two years," she said. "I don't even know what I'm doing tomorrow."

"I thought you wanted to study art."

"I might change my mind. Why? What about you?"

"My grandparents started a college fund for me, but I don't know. My dad never went to college, and he did okay." I laughed because it wasn't funny. "I'll probably just get a job. Drive a forklift or something."

"Seriously?"

"I don't want to think about it right now."

"Me neither."

I sometimes wondered if the only reason we were together was because there was nothing else pulling at us, like we were two solid planets in a universe of ghost planets, stuck in a tight orbit, together but not quite touching.

Gaia was thumbing another text.

"You ever think about why we're together?" I asked.

Gaia looked up at me so fast, it must've hurt her neck.

"Why?" she asked.

I shrugged. "I don't know. I just . . . Sometimes I feel like we're the only real people on earth, you know?"

"Maeve's real."

"Maeve is hundreds of miles away. She's pixels on your phone."

Gaia nodded, giving me a careful look.

"I just think you're the only person I know who gets me," I said.

"Do you get me?" she asked in a small voice.

I nodded, even though a lot of the time I didn't get her at all.

I was thinking about that during the two weeks before school started, when I noticed that she was taking a little longer to respond to my texts. Often when I called her, it would go to voice mail, and it'd be half an hour before she called me back. A half hour is a long time. Enough time for me to start thinking she was mad at me for something.

It didn't take much to make her mad. It took less all the time. Sometimes it took nothing at all, like the time we were at the mall. Gaia said she needed some clothes for school.

"What are we shopping for?" I asked.

"*I'm* shopping for jeans and boots. I don't know what *you're* shopping for."

"I'm not shopping for anything," I said, a bit startled by her tone.

"Then what are you doing here?"

"I guess just following you around," I said, trying to figure out what I'd done to piss her off.

She shrugged and headed toward DSW. At least she didn't tell me to go away. I watched her try on every pair of black boots in the store, everything from engineer boots like the ones she was wearing, to pointy-toed high-heeled boots that looked both painful and precarious. I made a couple of suggestions, which had the effect of her immediately ruling them out.

"Are you mad at me?" I asked as she was pulling on a pair of lizard-skin cowboy boots.

She gave me a side eye. "Should I be?"

"No. I mean, I don't think so."

She compressed her lips as if holding something in, then said, "I'm just really tired of talking about how everything sucks."

"But everything *does* suck," I said. I meant it to be a joke, but it didn't come out that way.

"I'm just sort of irritable."

I wondered if that meant she was having PMS, but I knew better than to ask.

"Do you want me to go?"

She tugged on the second boot and stood up. "What do you think?"

"Um . . . they don't suck?"

She laughed. "Nice try."

"Okay then. They suck."

"Really?" She turned this way and that, looking at the boots. "I kind of like them."

After that we were sort of okay again. She didn't buy the boots, but we had better luck in the jeans department at Macy's, where she bought two pairs of black jeans exactly like every other pair of jeans she owned. We walked around the mall and I made it a point to comment on things that didn't suck. It was funny for a while, but then Gaia clammed up and didn't have much to say, so we walked down to the Cineplex and she picked a movie that turned out to be so awful, we left halfway through. I walked her home, and the only thing we talked about was how much that movie sucked.

# "Choctaw Bingo"

## James McMurtry
## 8:48

**Columbia is right in the middle of Missouri.**
The guy drops me by a big McDonald's right next to the
freeway. He never told me his name, but I now know
every glorious detail of his perfect son's perfect life.

I go inside to use the bathroom, then order a fish
sandwich and a Coke. It's four in the afternoon
already, and Kansas City is still a couple hours' drive,
assuming I can hitch another ride. I eat quickly, then
head out to the I-70 on-ramp and stick my thumb out
and count the cars passing me by.

An hour later I'm at number 172 when a beat-
up old Ford Taurus drives past me. One brake light
comes on, and it pulls over about halfway down the
ramp. The car backs up toward me, one wheel on the

edge of the ramp, the other on the weedy shoulder. I jog toward it and meet it halfway. A woman in the passenger seat rolls down the window. She has wispy blonde hair and skin that looks dried out, as if she's been left out in the desert. I can't tell if she's in her twenties or her fifties.

"Need a ride?" she asks.

I nod, feeling a bit uneasy.

"Hop in," the male driver says.

"I'm going to Kansas City," I say.

"Cool," he says.

I think about how many cars passed me and didn't stop. If I don't take this ride, I could be here for hours. I take a breath, open the back door, and climb inside. I'm ankle-deep in empty Red Bull cans and Skittles wrappers. The car smells weird, like pancake syrup and Windex.

The driver pulls onto the freeway. He has blond hair too, and a couple of prominent zits on the back of his neck. I look at the rearview mirror. He's staring at me. His eyes are a muddy blue color, with red veins at the corners and dark pouches underneath.

"Kansas City, huh?" he says.

"Yeah. The part that's in Kansas."

"Kansas City, Kansas. Got a buddy lives there, right downtown. Helluva town. Got them good barbecue ribs, right, Honeypie?"

"That's for sure."

"Got them, what are they called? Jayhawks. Kansas

City Jayhawks. Kansas City Royals, Kansas City Chiefs, all kinds a sports. You like sports? Sure, you do. Everybody likes sports, right, Honeypie?"

"You got that right, Babe." She says it like it's his name. Both of them have hoarse voices.

"Saint Louie, KC, Oklahoma. Man, I been there, I been everywhere. Born in Texas, though. Texas born, Texas bred. Houston, Dallas, San Antone, Austin— man, that's one hell-raisin' town. Lubbock, Browns-ville, Amarillo—that means yellow in Mexican. Yellow, Texas. Who names a town after a color? Shreveport— that's Looseeana, right, Honeypie?"

"I ain't gonna argue, Babe."

"Been all the way to LA and every town in between. Albuquerque, Phoenix, Tucson, Casa Grande . . ." He keeps going, naming one city after another. I tune him out and look around the car. There are stubby bolts sticking out of the backs of the front seats, like some-thing used to be fastened there. The backseat is black vinyl, with lots of cuts and tears. The console between the front seats has holes drilled in it. Jammed into a hole in the dashboard is a radio that didn't come with the car. I try to roll down the back window a bit to let in some fresh air, but the button doesn't work, and the door handle is missing.

I'm starting to get very nervous.

" . . . Flagstaff, Vegas, Winslow . . ." The guy is still rattling off city names.

"Is this an old cop car?" I ask.

"Police Interceptor, baby. Got the four-point-six-liter V-8, heavy-duty suspension, the whole works, right, Honeypie?"

"Yeah, Babe."

He swerves across two lanes and takes the exit onto Stadium Boulevard.

"This is good," I say. "You can drop me here."

"Drop you? Ain't you going to Kansas City?"

"I changed my mind."

"We just got to make a pit stop at the Walmart. Have you in KC by suppertime." He turns left off the exit and heads south.

"Here's the deal. We need you to do us a little favor, okay? Just run into the Walmart and pick something up for us. You think you can do that?"

"Um . . . sure." Anything to get out of this car.

"You got any cash on you? Like, twenty bucks?"

"No."

"I bet you do, but it ain't no never mind. Honeypie can spot you."

A Walmart is coming up on the left. He pulls in and parks at the far edge of the lot. Honeypie is digging in her pockets. She comes out with a ten and a handful of ones. The guy grabs the money from her and turns to face me.

"Sudafed," he says. "Not the timed release, just the regular."

"Sudafed? You mean the stuff for when you have a cold or something?"

"Yeah. Honeypie and me, we got bad allergies."

"You got that right," Honeypie says.

"Twenty bucks' worth." He waves the money. "Don't worry. You don't need a prescription. Just a driver's license. You got a license, right?"

"Why?" I ask.

"The pharmacist will need your ID. They keep the Sudafed behind the counter."

"I mean, why do you want *me* to do it?"

"Because Missouri has this stupid law about how much you can buy, and me and Honeypie, we already bought our monthly max. They keep records, right? Goddamn police state. Only, here's the thing. You got to leave something with us. So you don't take our money and run, you dig?"

"I don't have anything," I tell him.

"You got shoes? Leave us your shoes."

I figure, why not? I can run in, buy the allergy medicine, come back and get my shoes, and then *not* get in the car.

I take off my shoes. He hands me the money. Honeypie gets out of the car and opens my door. She smiles, showing a gappy set of teeth that don't look so good.

"I'll be right back," I say, even though I'm not sure I will. I cross the parking lot in my stocking feet. There is a sign next to the door: NO SHIRT, NO SHOES, NO SERVICE. I ignore the sign and walk into the store.

A Walmart in Missouri is the same as a Walmart in Minnesota. I locate the pharmacy instantly and walk up to the window. A young woman looks up at me and raises her eyebrows.

"I need some . . . um . . . I need some Sudafed?"

"Sudafed? What kind, honey? We have twelve-hour, twenty-four-hour, multi-symptom, or just Sudafed."

"The regular kind."

"Box of twenty-four or forty-eight?"

"This much." I put the money on the counter.

"That's enough for two boxes of forty-eight," she says. "Why so much?"

"It's not for me. My . . . my mom sent me to get it."

"Okay. I'll need some form of identification."

I give her my driver's license. She sets it on her computer screen and starts typing in my name and number.

"You aren't a tweaker, are you, honey?"

"I don't even know what that is."

"You say this is for your mom? Does she use drugs?"

"No!"

"Lot of meth addicts buy Sudafed. That's why we keep it back here." She squints at her screen, taps a few keys. "Okay. I've got you in the database. That'll be seventeen thirty-six." She takes the money and gives me some change, and a few seconds later I'm walking out of the store.

I stop. The ex-cop-car has been joined by a real cop car, its lights flashing red and blue. Honeypie and Babe have their hands on the hood. They are being frisked. I stand and watch as the police handcuff the two of them, put them in the back of the squad car, and drive off. I wait a few more minutes, then cross the lot to their car. I look through the window. My shoes are in the backseat. I try all the doors. They're locked.

I walk back into the store. This time I'm stopped by a security guard.

"You need to get yourself a pair of shoes, you want to shop here," he says.

Part of me wants to blurt out the whole story, how I got kidnapped by a couple of meth addicts who forced me to give them my shoes, and then they got arrested, and my shoes were locked in their car. But that would lead to all sorts of questions.

"I need shoes," I say.

"I'll say you do!" The guard laughs.

"I mean, I came here to buy shoes. Mine got stolen."

The guard thinks for a moment, then shrugs and says, "Okay, then. Aisle twelve. But you better come out of here with something on your feet."

# "Holiday in Cambodia"

## The Dead Kennedys
## 4:39

**My new Walmart shoes look dorky as hell,** but they're dry and comfortable. I bought new socks, too. When I walk out of the store, the guard gives me a thumbs-up.

"Lookin' good, kid."

"Thanks," I say.

The tweakers' car is still there. I set the bag full of Sudafed on the hood. It was their money. Maybe they'll be back.

The freeway is about half a mile away. By the time I get there, it's almost six o'clock. I'm not too excited about hitching a ride that'll land me in Kansas City after dark. There's a hotel nearby, the Rest Stop Inn, with a sign that says $39.99.

As I enter the lobby, I can see right away why it's so cheap. The carpet is worn, the potted plant is plastic, and the guy behind the chipped, fake-wood counter hasn't shaved in a week. I ask him for a room. He looks me up and down and says, "How many?"

"Just one room," I say.

"I mean how many of you are there?"

"Just me. For one night."

"I have a room with two queen beds, second floor, sixty-five dollars."

"It says thirty-nine on your sign."

"That room's taken."

"That's false advertising!"

"I'm not in charge of the sign, kid. And I don't set the rates."

"You don't have anything cheaper?"

"Nope."

We stare at each other for a couple of seconds. Then he says, "Look, kid, if you're a Triple-A member, I can knock off six bucks. I won't ask you to prove it."

I don't know what "triple A" is, but I nod. It's not like I have a lot of options. I hand him Mom's credit card. He looks at it and says, "Your name's Amanda?"

"That's my mom," I say.

He shrugs and runs it through his machine. A few seconds later he frowns and tosses the card back on the counter.

"Looks like Amanda canceled her card."

○ ○ ○

I leave the hotel with no idea what to do. Was it just a few days ago I left home? Back then I didn't know where I was going or what I was going to do, and I liked it. Back then it felt like freedom; now it feels like a trap.

I could have paid cash for the room, but that would have used up a quarter of all the money I have left. I have two choices. I can find a park, or someplace with bushes to hide in, wrap myself up in discarded newspapers and Bran's hoodie, and wait for morning. Or I can go stand on the entrance ramp with my thumb out and hope for a ride. The thought of arriving in Kansas City in the dead of night is not appealing, and I sure don't want to catch a ride from another car full of meth heads. I probably won't be able to find Prairie Village until tomorrow in any case.

I walk, my thoughts going in circles, until I come to a huge mall with a Taco Bell in the parking lot. That sets off my hunger pangs, so I invest five dollars in a combo meal: a taco, a gordita, a burrito, a bag of cinnamon twists, and a Dew. I sit in a booth and eat slowly, hardly tasting the food. I can't believe my mom canceled the credit card. Yes, I can. But now what does she expect me to do?

What do homeless people do? I've seen them in parks, under bridges, or just walking. Do they eat at Taco Bell? Do they eat scraps out of dumpsters? I don't know anything about surviving on my own without a car and a credit card. Allie and Randy and Bran got along okay by stealing food and, in Bran's case, stealing my car. Also, they had all that camping gear.

I'm not exactly destitute, but I sure *feel* destitute. Maybe there's a bus station nearby. I wonder what it would cost to take a Greyhound. I take out my iPod. There's no Wi-Fi at this Taco Bell, and my iPod battery is down to 10 percent. I finish my last cinnamon twist and head for the mall.

A few minutes later I've found what I'm looking for: a fifteen-dollar charger from Target, and a Wi-Fi signal at the Starbucks. I buy a small coffee, load it up with cream and sugar, and then plug the charger into an outlet next to one of the tables and search for a Greyhound station in Columbia. I find it right away. It's about four miles away. I should be able to walk there in an hour or two. The next bus to Kansas City doesn't leave until tomorrow morning. I sip my coffee, making it last. I wait for the iPod to get up to 50 percent, then plug in my earbuds and start walking in my Walmart shoes while getting my ears shredded by some old band called the Dead Kennedys.

# Calculus

**A week before Labor Day, Gaia went up to** a resort on Lake Vermilion with her dad and her brother. She said it was something they did every year. It was the first time since we'd met that I'd gone more than a day without seeing her. She wasn't coming back until Labor Day, and the day after that was the first day of school. It was also my birthday.

Gaia and I texted a few times while she was gone, but she had to paddle a canoe halfway across the lake to get a cell signal because the resort was in the middle of nowhere. I guess it must be hard to text from a canoe, because she didn't have much to say. Her brother caught a bunch of walleyes. It was cold at night. She got bit by a horsefly.

The last text I got was the Friday before Labor Day. She said she'd seen a moose, and her battery was almost dead and she'd forgotten to bring her charger. I texted back for her to call me as soon as she got home. I don't know if the text went through.

I didn't hear from her on Labor Day. I walked over to her house after dinner, but they weren't home yet. That night I called her at least a dozen times. Nothing.

In the morning I talked my mom into letting me use her car to drive to school the first day.

"It's my birthday," I reminded her. It took a lot of whining, but she finally agreed.

I had a plan. Gaia and I would skip school and spend the whole day together, just the two of us. I got there early and waited outside where the buses unload. When Gaia's bus arrived, she didn't get off.

She must have missed it, I thought. Or maybe she had caught a ride from someone. I tried calling her. I sent her a text. No answer either way. I decided I might as well go to class—there was no point in skipping if I couldn't do it with Gaia. Maybe she was already in school.

All through first period I kept sneaking looks at my phone. No reply.

Between classes I asked a bunch of people who knew her. No one had seen her.

I was getting worried. What if she was sick? What if she'd had a car accident?

I went into second period—calculus—in a sort of
daze. I had signed up for it because I'd thought Gaia
would be impressed.

Jason Herter was sitting across from me. Jason was
one of Saint Andrew Valley's resident geniuses, and
also a total asshole.

"*Gabel?*" he said. "What're *you* doing in calc? Didn't
you practically flunk trig?"

"Yeah, but I made up for it at Screw U," I said,
which made no sense at all, but Jason was a total
priss-butt, and I knew it would shut him up. He was
right, though. I had no head for math. I basically spent
the whole period tuning out Mr. Nestor and peeking
at my phone.

At least, I did until Nestor's snappish voice cut
through my haze.

"Mr. Gabel!"

I looked up. He was holding out his hand.

"Your phone, please!"

He waggled his fingers. I imagined three months of
listening to him drone on about calculus, then stood
up and put the phone in my pocket.

"*Mr. Gabel!*"

I walked out of the room. I half expected him to
come chasing after me, but he didn't. Why should he
care? He was probably relieved I was gone.

On the way to Gaia's house I thought up a hundred
reasons why she wasn't texting me back. Lost phone.

Stolen phone. Battery dead. Phone confiscated by her dad. Deathly ill. Mad at me for something. Cell tower out. Fingers slammed in door. . . . I cycled from angry to scared to hopeless to worried and back again, and by the time I got there, I was a complete mess.

I rang the doorbell. It took about half a minute for the door to open. It felt like an eternity.

It was Derek, but not the confident, smiling, friendly Derek I was used to. This Derek greeted me with a blank, unwelcoming look.

"Oh," he said. "Gabel."

"I'm looking for Gaia," I said.

He just stared at me, and my stomach started floating like coming up over the top of the highest hill on a roller coaster.

"She wasn't in school and she's not getting my texts," I said.

"Wait here," he said, and half closed the door. I stood where I was for a minute, then another minute, heading downhill on an infinitely high roller coaster.

The door opened. I almost didn't recognize her. She was wearing a light blue cotton sweater. She did have her new black jeans on, but instead of her usual black boots, she wore blue leather sneakers.

"Gaia?" I said.

She looked straight at me. She was wearing no makeup at all, and she didn't smile.

I moved toward her. Her eyes watched me coming.

"Are you okay?" I asked.

She smiled, but it wasn't quite the smile I'd been hoping for.

"I'm fine," she said, and took my hand.

"You look different. I mean, you look great. I like it."

She squeezed my hand, then let go.

"New year, new look." She stepped outside and sat down on the steps. I sat next to her, not quite touching because I was afraid if I did, she'd move away.

"You weren't in school," I said.

She nodded, staring at a box-elder bug crawling across the sidewalk a few feet in front of us.

"I've been texting," I said. My voice sounded shaky and far away.

"I know."

"I walked out of calculus."

I thought she'd ask me to explain, but she just pressed her lips together.

"It's my birthday," I said.

Her face seemed to shrink in on itself.

"I'm sorry," she said in a voice so small, I could barely hear her. "I'm changing schools," she said.

"What? Why?"

"I'm moving."

I wasn't sure I'd heard her right. Had she said *"moving"*?

"Moving where?"

"I'm going to stay with Maeve."

"But . . . didn't she move to Wisconsin?"

Gaia nodded, still watching the bug on the sidewalk.

"Gaia?"

She turned her head and looked at me. You know that look a person gets when they are crying but have no tears? I saw it on my mom after Dad died, like her heart, brain, and face had completely disconnected.

That was what I saw on Gaia.

She said, in the flattest, driest voice imaginable, "I have to go."

She stood up and went back inside and closed the door softly. The click of the latch sounded like a gunshot.

# "In the Cold, Cold Night"

## The White Stripes
## 2:58

**I get to the Greyhound station after dark.** It's not a regular bus station. The sign on the building says MIDWAY TRAVEL PLAZA. There are no buses, just some cars out front, and a couple dozen semis parked in back. It's more like a truck stop. The travel plaza has a restaurant, with a bar and a tattoo parlor called Under the Gun on the second floor. There's a cowboy boot store behind the building, and a Budget Inn across the parking lot.

I think I must be in the wrong place, but after walking around a bit, I spot a blue-and-silver Greyhound sign hanging on the wall next to the restaurant. A waitress in the restaurant assures me that I'm in the right place, and tells me I can buy a ticket in the convenience store.

I buy a ticket for the morning bus, then wonder what I'm going to do for the next twelve hours. There isn't anything resembling a waiting area. The restaurant is open twenty-four hours, but I don't think they'd want me sleeping there. I cross the parking lot to the hotel and go inside. It's even cheaper-looking than the last hotel, and I'm a little relieved when the guy at the counter tells me they're booked.

Back outside, I walk over to the cowboy boot store just for something to do. Not that I'm in the market for boots. Anyway, it's closed.

Back at the travel center, the bar upstairs is blasting country western music. Three guys and two girls are standing under a light outside the restaurant, smoking. I check my iPod for the time. Ten thirty. The bus is at nine forty-five in the morning. Eleven hours and fifteen minutes to go.

In the store where I bought the bus ticket, I kill half an hour looking at T-shirts, trucker caps, and key chains. I buy a bag of smoked almonds and go back outside. The music from upstairs is louder, and the lights are on in the tattoo parlor. I think about getting a tat. On my forehead. *Life Sucks and Then You Die.* I think about what it would cost, and how much it would hurt. Maybe not.

I walk around to the back and sit on the asphalt

with my back to the wall and eat my almonds slowly, one at a time, chewing each one to paste before swallowing it. I look at my iPod. It's a few minutes after eleven.

At eleven thirty I go into the restaurant. The woman at the cash register gives me a blank look and waves her hand at all the empty tables.

"Wherever you like, honey. It ain't like we're busy." She looks like she might be about forty, or maybe older.

The only other customer is a skinny old long-haired guy at the counter hunched over his plate. He has his left arm wrapped around the plate like he's afraid somebody's going to steal it. His other arm is shoveling biscuits and gravy into the hole between his beard and his mustache. I don't think he has any teeth, but it's hard to tell.

I sit at one of the booths along the opposite wall. Above the booth is a display of old hubcaps. I look over the menu. Biscuits and gravy is three ninety-nine, but I don't want that. The woman—I guess she's the waitress—is sitting on her stool scrolling through her phone. I'm in no hurry—I plan to sit in this booth for as long as they'll let me—but it seems kind of rude that she's ignoring me.

Several minutes pass. I read the menu, looking for something that will take me a long time to eat. Finally she puts her phone away, hikes her butt off the stool, and walks over to me. The way she walks, I'm guessing she's older than I thought.

"What can I get for you, honey?" She sounds tired.

I haven't decided. I ask her if I can have a Coke while I peruse the menu. I actually said "peruse." I didn't even know I knew that word.

"Pepsi okay, hon?"

I say that's fine. I *peruse* the menu some more and decide on a cheeseburger and fries for seven ninety-nine. While I'm waiting, another customer comes in, a younger guy, maybe thirty. His black hair is sticking out from under a Jayhawks ball cap, and the sleeves of his blue sweatshirt are pushed up. His forearms are covered with tattoos. He hasn't shaved for a few days. I touch my face. I haven't shaved since I left Minnesota, but on me it doesn't matter so much.

The waitress is coming toward me with my Pepsi. He catches her eye, and his face transforms into a world-class smile that makes Allie's smile look like nothing. His whole face goes into it. The waitress can't help but smile back.

"How you doing tonight?" he asks her. I get the feeling he isn't just making a polite noise; he really wants to know.

"I'm getting by, doll." She stands up a little straighter and touches her hair. "How are you?"

"Fantastic!" he says. "I'm a little hungry, though. You think you could help me out with that? Maybe a cup of coffee to start?"

"Sure thing. You just sit yourself down however you like, and I'll be with you in a jiff."

He watches her set my Pepsi in front of me. He looks right at me, smiles, and nods. It's impossible not to smile and nod back. He looks over the room and checks out the long-haired guy at the counter.

"Hey, how's it going?" he says.

The guy at the counter gives the newcomer a suspicious look and shrugs.

"How them biscuits?" the new guy asks.

"I had worse," the guy at the counter says.

The new guy laughs, and gets a gaping smile out of the counter guy. Turns out he has teeth after all. Two of them.

The new guy looks over the tables and chooses one in the middle. The waitress pours his coffee as he is sitting down. She starts pouring with the pot close to the cup, and as she pours, she raises the pot up about two feet, then brings it back down.

"I like the way you pour!" the guy says.

"Never spill a drop," she says proudly.

"What's your name, gorgeous?"

The waitress giggles, which is a strange thing to hear from an older woman.

"I'm Jill," she says.

The guy grins. "Perfect!" he exclaims. "My name's Jack! Jack and Jill!"

Jack and Jill laugh as if their names are the most wonderful things in the world. To my surprise, I'm smiling too.

Jack orders breakfast, even though it's almost

midnight. He doesn't even look at the menu. "Two eggs over easy, bacon, sausage, a couple of them biscuits. . . . You have grapefruit juice?"

"We sure do!" She is delighted to be taking his order.

"Fantastic! And a short stack of pancakes."

She takes his order back to the kitchen. He sips his coffee, then looks over at me.

"Excellent coffee!"

I don't know how to respond, so I just smile back at him and nod.

"I love these old-school truck stops! And this one even has a bar upstairs."

"Are you a trucker?" I ask.

He grins. I think he must be the happiest guy I've ever met.

"Lost my license," he says happily. "But I get around."

The waitress, Jill, returns with his grapefruit juice.

"Perfect!" he says. "Thank you!"

The waitress beams. I wait for her to look at me so I can order, but it's like I'm invisible. She goes back to the kitchen to oversee the rest of Jack's excellent fantastic perfect breakfast.

I think I should hate this guy, but I don't.

"Do you live around here?" I ask.

"Yes! Well, Kansas City. I was just down in Jeff City visiting my brother Trent. He's in prison, but he'll be out in five years. That's not so bad, right?"

"I guess it's better than ten years."

"Truth!" His face goes slack, and it's like the lights dimmed. It lasts only for a second. He sips his excellent coffee, and his smile returns. "Heading home tomorrow to see my girl. Prettiest girl in the state!"

"On the morning Greyhound?"

"Yes!"

"Me too."

"Fantastic!"

Jill appears with two plates and sets them before him. He tells her how fantastic everything looks.

"How late is that bar open?" he asks.

"One, but they usually keep serving until two."

"Plenty of time!" he says with a grin.

"You enjoy your breakfast, doll." Jill pats Jack on his shoulder, then notices me staring at her and comes up to my booth. "What can I get you, honey?" I'm pretty sure "doll" ranks higher than "honey."

I order the cheeseburger and fries. While I wait, I watch Jack eat. He enjoys every bite, with lots of lip-smacking and *mmmm*. By the time my food arrives, Jack has finished his late-night breakfast. He radiates contentment, as if he's just eaten a ten-course meal in the finest restaurant on the planet.

My cheeseburger has no cheese, and the french fries are limp.

"That looks fantastic!" Jack says. I think for a moment that he is being sarcastic, but he's not. "Nothing like a truck stop burger!"

I take a bite. It's pretty good.

○ ○ ○

It's a long night. Jill lets me hang out in the restaurant for a couple hours. Jack put her in a good mood, and even after he leaves, she seems happy. Other customers come and go: a couple of weary-looking truckers, a drunk guy from the bar upstairs, and two women dressed in skin-tight jeans, halter tops, and thick layers of makeup. I fall asleep in the booth for a while. I can't help it. I didn't sleep so good last night, with rain seeping into my tent and me thinking about my car being gone.

It's one o'clock when Jill shakes my shoulder. I was dreaming about Gaia. In my dream she wanted to show me a two-headed cow, and we went inside this barn that had glass doors like an office building, and my dad was standing there, but he didn't recognize me.

"Honey, I'm going off shift in a minute," Jill says in a low voice. "Daryl over there is taking over." She points with her chin. Daryl, a slouchy, sour-faced fellow, is sorting through the cash register. There are no other customers. "You're going to have to order more food if you want to keep holding down this booth," the waitress says.

I'm still half in my dream, but I think I understand what she's saying.

"Uh . . . okay. A cup of coffee?"

"How about a piece of pie with that?"

"Sure."

I take about an hour to eat the pie. Daryl keeps giving me the stink eye, and he won't refill my coffee after the third time, so I pay my bill and go back outside.

It's gotten colder. I zip up Bran's hoodie and pull the hood over my head. The bar upstairs is closing, and the last few customers walk unsteadily down the stairs and head back to their trucks or the hotel. Jack comes down last, wearing a loose, crooked smile. He stumbles past without noticing me and weaves across the parking lot to the hotel.

I stand there listening to the hum of traffic from the freeway and wondering how I'm going to pass the rest of the night. After a while I walk over to the hotel, hoping they'll let me sit in the lobby for a while. The door dings when I enter. No one is behind the desk. I sit down in the tiny lobby on a cracked vinyl couch between a fake palm tree and a rack of brochures, and look for a Wi-Fi signal on my iPod. There's a signal, but I need a password.

A minute later a sleepy irritated-looking fellow comes out from the back room and asks me if I'm a guest.

I think of that guy Jack, and I force my face to smile. "I tried to be," I say. "I was here before, remember?" He clearly doesn't. I'm not even sure he's the same guy. "But you didn't have a room. Is it okay if I just hang out here for a while?"

He examines my smile, thinks for a second, then says, "Lobby's for guests only."

"I'm kind of stuck here, waiting for the bus." I give my smile all I've got. "I won't be any bother."

He sighs and looks at the clock. Three a.m.

"A couple hours," he says. "But I want you gone when our guests start checking out."

"Fantastic!" I say.

Five minutes later I'm slumped on the vinyl sofa sleeping like the dead.

# Blocked

**The day Gaia told me she was leaving, I got** back in Mom's car and drove, around and around, going nowhere, carrying with me a storm in my head. That was the day the moonfaced cop gave me the ticket. I texted Gaia over and over again, and all that night, but got no response until five thirty the next morning: Number unavailable.

She'd *blocked* me.

I think I went a little crazy. I took my mom's car without asking her—she was still sleeping. I didn't even change out of the sweats and T-shirt I'd slept in.

The sun hadn't risen yet, and Gaia's house was dark. I rang the doorbell. Nothing. I banged on the door. Nothing. I walked around the back and banged on her window. I went back to the front door and started kicking it. A light came on inside. I waited.

Derek opened the door. His hair was all messed up, and he had on his pajamas.

"Gabel," he said. "What the hell?"

"Sorry if I woke you up." I forced myself to speak clearly, although all I wanted to do was scream in his face. "I need to talk to Gaia."

"She's not here."

"Where is she?"

"She's gone."

"To Wisconsin?"

"She didn't tell you?"

"Not really. She said she was going to stay with Maeve. But I don't have the phone number there. Or an address. Or anything."

Derek pressed his lips together the way Gaia did when she was about to say something I didn't want to hear.

"I'm not going to get in the middle of this," he said after a moment.

"In the middle of *what*?" My voice cracked.

"Sorry." He shut the door. I stared at it for a second, then kicked it, twice, really hard. The door swung open.

"Gabel, if you keep kicking this door, I'm going to come out there and kick your ass."

The way he said it was weird, like he wasn't really mad; he was simply, wearily, stating a fact. I believed him, and when he closed the door, I turned and walked back to the car. My legs felt like wood. I drove home.

Naturally, my mom was furious about me taking her car without permission, but I didn't care. I sat through her whole what-were-you-thinking routine without feeling a thing. I watched her talking at me, and it was like watching a video, as if I was seeing the world through a screen. I didn't hear anything she said until she got right in my face and yelled, "Look at you! You're not even dressed for school! You'll miss your bus!"

I looked at the clock. "I already missed it," I said. "Anyways, I'm not going."

"Not an option," she said. "I won't have you lazing about the house all day long on your second day of school. I'll drive you."

It was easier to go along with it than it was to argue, so I went to my room and changed out of the sweats and tee into jeans and a different shirt.

When we got there—the whole trip spent in icy silence—Mom waited in her car and watched to make sure I went into the school. Once inside I wasn't sure what to do. I didn't have my schedule. I definitely wasn't going back to Nestor's calc class. I thought about walking back out. Instead I went to the office and told them I'd gone home sick the day before, and I was dropping calculus, and I had nowhere to go.

In a way, life is easier in the zombie zone. You just go where people tell you and pretend to do whatever it is they want you to do. I sat in the office until second period, then went to American Literature, then biology, then to the cafeteria, where I bought a bag of chips and sat with Garf and listened to him tell me about some new comic book artist he liked. After a few minutes he gave me a funny look and asked me if I was okay.

"Yeah, why?" I said.

"You seem sort of . . . not there," he said.

"I'm fine."

"So you really dropped calculus?"

"Yeah. I replaced it with a class called Practical Math."

"That's what all the jocks take, right?"

"I guess."

"Like, if you're on the twelve-yard line and you gain forty yards on a passing play but get a ten-yard penalty, how far do you have to kick the ball for a field goal?"

"Exactly."

He didn't say anything for a few seconds. I finished my chips. I figured he wanted to ask me about Gaia, and I didn't want to talk about Gaia, so I got up and went to my next class, something called Theories of Justice. I didn't remember signing up for it, and I had no idea what it was about. An hour later, when the bell rang, I still didn't know, and I didn't care.

*Gaia met another guy. A guy smarter than me and better-looking and taller and who would drink a*

*Black Mamba and never complain. Or it was that day when I wouldn't sit on the bench or tell her why and I just walked away. Or Gaia's dad sent her away because he hates me. Or Gaia thinks I'm stupid because I wanted to climb up onto the big blue chicken. Or I have really bad breath and she couldn't bear to tell me. Or she never really liked me; she just hung out with me because she was bored. Because she felt sorry for me. Because I'm so pathetic. Gaia thinks I'm a wimp because I couldn't save her from Ben Gingrass. Gaia is a secret lesbian and she's in love with Maeve. She thinks my Darth Vader collection is stupid. Somebody told Gaia something about me that wasn't true. I'm too boring for her. I'm not arty enough. I'm creepy and weird. I have no friends except Garf, and he's weird too. When she thinks about me, she rolls her eyes and shakes her head. She's telling Maeve what a loser I am. I wasn't nice to Maeve. She—*

"Steven Gabel!"

I looked up. Mr. Hallgren was laser beaming me with his squinty black eyes.

"What are you doing?"

I was sitting in study hall with a dozen other losers. Last period of the day. Everybody was looking at me.

"Nothing," I said.

"Precisely," Hallgren said. "This is not stare-vacantly-into-space hall. This is *study* hall. At the very least you could open a book and *pretend* to read."

I shrugged and opened a random book to a random page. *Everyday Mathematics—Making Numbers Fun.* The chapter was called "How to Balance a Checking Account." Fun! Who uses checks anymore? I flipped forward, all the way to the back, where I found a section called "Interesting Numbers." The section had been misnamed, unless you happened to be interested in things like the number of acres of cornfields in Iowa, or the age of the oldest living hippopotamus. One thing did catch my eye. In the United States there are 105 teenage males to every 100 teen females. It did not say how many Stiggys there are for every Gaia.

I let the words blur. I talked to Gaia for the first time on May 7. I got us kicked out of Wigglesworth's three days later. We had sex on the Fourth of July. I add up the days. Fifty-eight days from talking in the McDonald's to getting naked in my room. *Practical Math.* Sixty-three days later, here I am staring at a remedial math book, and she is gone. One hundred twenty-one days total.

Fun!

# "America"

## Simon and Garfunkel
## 3:37

**The motel clerk pokes my shoulder, and I** wake up with a start. At first I think only a few minutes have passed, but then I feel how stiff my neck is and realize I've been asleep for a while.

"Time to move on, son," he says.

The clock behind the desk reads 5:41. It's still dark out. I stand up and stretch.

"My shift's up in twenty. Can't have Carla show up and find a vagrant camping in her lobby." He smiles to show me he's kidding. Sort of. I guess I *am* sort of a vagrant.

"You want to take a cup with you?" He gestures at the coffee machine.

"Sure. Thanks. And thanks for letting me camp out here." I fill a paper cup with coffee.

"Supposed to be a nice day. Chilly last night, but it's warming up now."

I stir in a creamer and a couple of sugars.

"I been there," he says.

"Been where?" I really don't know what he's talking about.

"In between. Still there, in a way. Columbia. You know what Columbia is? Halfway between Kansas City and Saint Louis. In between. Which way you going?"

"Kansas City," I say.

"Good luck."

I'm in the middle of Missouri, I'm running low on money, and I have no idea whether I'll find Bran and my car when I get to Kansas City. For all I know, he drove it to Florida or California—but I'm feeling pretty good. It helps that the motel clerk was nice to me. Maybe my asshole magnetism isn't working.

The bus shows up right on time. Several passengers get out, and I get on. I pick a window seat in the middle. A minute later the happy guy from the restaurant gets on, only he doesn't look so happy. His face is slack, and his eyes are red and framed with dark circles of bruised-looking flesh. He is carrying a large cup of coffee and a small overnight bag. He sits across the aisle from me and doesn't say anything. I don't think he's noticed me. He seems pretty focused on drinking his coffee, so I leave him alone.

The passengers who got off the bus to use the restrooms and buy snacks get back on, and a few minutes later the bus rolls out of the parking lot. It's only a third full. I rest my forehead against the window and stare out at the world passing by.

We've been on the road for about half an hour when I get this crawly feeling like a bug is about to land on me. I turn my head and see Jack smiling at me.

"How you doing?" he says.

"Pretty good."

He leans across the aisle and holds out his hand. "Dave Quigley."

"Stiggy." I shake his hand. "I thought your name was Jack."

"Jack?" He seems confused.

"Uh, yeah. From that restaurant last night?"

"Oh!" He smiles. His smile is twenty-four karat, but it looks like it hurts. "Sure! You had that burger and fries! Sorry. Rough night. I just told that waitress I was Jack so we could be Jack and Jill. She liked it. Real name's Dave, though. You going to KC?"

"Prairie Village, actually."

That makes him laugh. "Perfect Village!" he says. "Should've known, with that polo shirt and the KC hoodie. You look like a Cake."

That was what Bran called me.

"What's that?" I ask.

"Cake. When I was in high school, that's what we called guys from Prairie Village: Cake Eaters."

"Yeah, well I'm not from there. I just have to pick up my car."

"You got a car? How come you're riding the big gray dog?"

"This guy borrowed it. Without permission."

"Stole it, huh?"

"Yeah."

He laughs. I don't see the humor in it, but I laugh too.

After that we don't talk. Dave stares out his window and I stare out mine, looking at the different colors of the fields: some green, some brown, some yellow. I try to figure out what the crops are. The only one I know for sure is the corn. After a while I fall asleep and don't wake up until we pull into the Greyhound station in Kansas City.

# Shoes

**One day—this was three weeks after Gaia** left—I just didn't go to school. I took the bus, but when I got there, I couldn't make myself go inside. Instead I walked. I walked to places I used to go with Gaia. I'd been doing that a lot lately. I even drove out to the mushroom caves one afternoon, but I didn't go inside. I went back to the Minneapolis Sculpture Garden too, and stood in front of that bronze woman stepping out of a dead wolf and tried to see it the way Gaia had seen it.

I guess you'd call it wallowing. Slogging my way through the miserable muck inside my head. The day I decided not to go back to school, I walked over to Wigglesworth's, determined to order a Black Mamba and drink the whole disgusting thing. Of course, the same girl was working, and as soon as she saw me come in, she whipped out her phone, so I left.

The odd thing was that a part of me welcomed each little jolt of pain.

Back in the eighth grade I had a friend named Aiden Invie who was into stabbing himself with this safety pin. He always carried that pin with him. He'd even do it in school, poking his thighs through his jeans, always walking around with bloody dots on his pants. Back then I didn't get why he would stab himself, but I guess now I was doing the same thing—hurting myself to cut through the numbness, to make the aching vacuum stop for just a moment. Aiden moved to Saint Paul in the ninth grade, so I don't know if he bled to death or what.

After Wigglesworth's I walked over to East River Park and imagined I was my father. I moved from bench to bench and forced myself to sit on all of them and look out over the river and think about how it had looked to him in February. I was pretty sure I knew which bench he'd picked—the one with the best view—but when I sat on it, it felt the same as all the others. Cold dead metal.

I walked from there to Gaia's house, but I didn't stop. Didn't even look at it except out of the corner of my eye. I circled the block and walked past it again, and again.

I must have walked twenty miles that day. When

I got home, I had a huge blister on my right heel. I popped it with a safety pin and watched the water trickle out.

Mom had left a note for me. She was at her Zumba class. I didn't know what Zumba was. Some sort of exercise.

I went out to the garage and started the Mustang and listened to some N.W.A. I imagined myself backing out of the garage onto the street and going. Just driving. The fact that I didn't have any place to go didn't bother me—it was kind of the whole point.

I turned the car off and went to my room and started filling a cardboard box with all my Star Wars junk: my lightsaber, the TIE fighter Geoff had busted, the variously sized Darth figurines including the big one Dad had given me for my eighth birthday, and Wonder Woman. I threw in my PlayStation, too. Then I called Garf.

Brain Food was only eight blocks away, but the box was heavy and I had to set it down a bunch of times to rest. When I got there, Garf was waiting out front with his skateboard, practicing ollies, trying to jump the curb. Garf had been trying to master the ollie for years. He wasn't very good at it.

I noticed he was wearing a brand-new pair of Adidas skate shoes. That surprised me because Garf was not big on spending money.

He saw me coming and kicked up his board.

"You sure you want to do this?" he said.

"I'm sure."

"I told Tobias you were coming. He's in a mood."

"Tobias is *always* in a mood," I said.

We went inside. Tobias was definitely in a mood.

"More junk," he said. "Just what I need."

It took Tobias half an hour to go through everything. He rejected the PlayStation. "Three years old? I could pick that up at any garage sale for a buck." He went through all my Vader stuff, setting the figurines aside one by one, saying, "Junk. Junk. Junk." He paused when he got to the TIE fighter, examined it, saw the crack, set it aside. "Junk."

Wonder Woman was a different story. I could see his beady little eyes light up.

"Well, well, well," he said, fondling the unopened box.

"It was my mom's," I said.

He sat back in his chair and said, "So, what do you want?"

"What will you pay me?" I asked.

"It's mostly junk." He waved his hand dismissively. "But then, I'm in the junk business. Four hundred for the lot."

"Four hundred!" Garf said. "The Wonder Woman alone is worth more than a thousand!"

Tobias snorted. "In your dreams, kid."

"It's mint!" Garf said.

"Mint, schmint. At auction you *might* get a thou,

but probably not. Keep in mind you got to give 30 percent to the auction house. And I got my markup to consider. I put it on display here, I *might* ask six hundred, and most likely it'd sit on display for a year before some collector spots it and offers me four."

"What about all the Star Wars stuff?" Garf said.

"Dime a dozen." He puffed out his cheeks and said, "Tell you what. You guys have been coming here a long time. I could go five hundred for the lot."

"Don't do it," Garf said to me.

"How about for everything except Wonder Woman?" I asked.

"Not interested."

"Don't do it," Garf said. "Seriously."

"How about for just the Wonder Woman?" I asked.

Tobias shrugged. "I could go three."

"I'll give you four," Garf said.

I looked at Garf, completely surprised. "Since when do you have four hundred bucks?"

"I have money," he said. "Investment capital."

"What the hell?" Tobias said, his face turning pink. "You come in here asking me to buy your junk, and now it's a bidding war?"

Garf said, "Well, you won't pay what it's worth."

Tobias jumped to his feet. "Get the hell out!" His face had gone from pink to a scary shade of red. "Both of you, and your junk, too!"

Outside, Garf stopped and took off his shoes and socks. He stuffed the socks into the shoes.

"Why are you doing that?" I asked.

"New shoes." He tied the laces together and hung them over his shoulder. "I want the soles to stay sticky."

"I ever tell you you're weird?"

"All the time."

On the way to his house, I tried to talk him into buying all of it.

"You could sell the Vaders online," I said.

"So could you."

"Yeah, but I'm leaving."

"Yeah, right." He didn't believe me.

We got to his house, a rambler on Tenth Street, and went through the side door into his bedroom. One thing about Garf, he had the neatest, most organized bedroom I'd ever seen. He put Wonder Woman on a shelf next to his BB-8, then took a cigar box from his dresser drawer. He opened the top. It was full of money.

"Garf! Dude! You're rich!"

He sorted through the bills and counted out four hundred dollars, all in twenties. There was plenty left.

"Four hundred, right?" he said as he handed them to me.

"Yeah . . . Um . . . where'd you get all the cash?"

"Here and there. You know, I mow almost every lawn on the block."

"You do?" I'd had no idea. "But you never spend any money. You're the cheapest guy I know!"

"That's how come I can afford to buy your Wonder Woman. I'll probably sell it on eBay."

"Whatever." I picked up my box of junk. "See you."

Garf followed me outside with his skateboard under one arm and his new shoes slung over his shoulder.

"Where are you going?" I asked.

"Park."

The skateboard park was on the way to my house.

Neither of us spoke for the first block. I was irritated about him planning to sell Wonder Woman. I'd been thinking he bought the doll because he wanted to help me out, and because he liked Wonder Woman. But it turns out it was just a business deal for him, a way to fill up his cigar box with more money.

"How much are you going to sell it for?" I asked him.

Garf shrugged. "I'll have to do some research."

"I didn't know you were such a wheeler-dealer."

"It's not like you know anything about me."

He had a point. We'd been friends for six or seven months, but most of the time we just talked about comics and movies and games. I supposed there were things he didn't know about me, too.

"I mean, you spent practically the whole summer with Gaia."

*Thud.* Why did he have to mention her name?

"And now that she's dumped you, we're hanging out again."

I wanted to tell him to shut up, but I didn't say anything. My chest felt all bubbly, like there was an explosion building inside my rib cage.

"Where'd she go, anyway?"

"I don't know." My voice sounded as if it was somebody else talking.

"You don't know?"

"She's staying with Maeve."

"Maeve Samms? Didn't she move to a farm or something?"

"How do you know that?"

"I just do. What did you do to piss her off, anyway?"

That did it. I dropped the box. Plastic rattled, matching the sound in my head. Garf, surprised, stopped walking. I snatched the shoes off his shoulder, swung them once, and sent them flying like a bola, end over end. It was a perfect throw, even though I hadn't been aiming. They hit a power line and wrapped around it, then hung there swinging, thirty feet up, sticky rubber soles bouncing off each other.

Garf stared up at his shoes, his mouth hanging open.

I picked up my box of junk and upended it. Darth Vaders hit the sidewalk with a noisy clatter. I threw the empty box out onto the street.

"Sell them on eBay," I said. My voice sounded shaky and far away. "Buy yourself a new pair of shoes."

# "Fast Car"

## Tracy Chapman
## 4:57

**The Kansas City Greyhound depot is in an** industrial area. I get off the bus still half-asleep. Dave steps out right behind me. We both stand there looking around. I'm trying to figure out which way is south. Prairie Village is about eight miles away. I'll have to walk.

"You got a ride coming?" Dave asks.

"No, I'm walking," I tell him. "Do you know which way Prairie Village is?"

He points, then says, "My girl is picking me up. We could give you a lift if you want."

"Sure!" My luck must be changing. "Thank you!"

"She should be here anytime now. You'll like her. Pam's great!"

Dave and I grab some drinks and snacks from the vending machines inside and wait in the parking lot. Dave watches the cars coming down the street. He's smiling, but his brow is furrowed. He reminds me of a worried dog waiting for his master to get home.

"How do you stay so happy all the time?" I ask him.

"What do you mean?"

"You're so positive. I'm kind of jealous. Like with that waitress last night. She was a total sourpuss until you showed up, and then she got all cheerful."

"If people think you're glad to see them, they're nicer. If you act like you think they're nice, they act nice to you. *Nice makes nice*, that's what my mom always told me."

"I think I'm the opposite. The people I meet always turn out to be assholes. I'm an asshole magnet."

He laughs as if I've just made the funniest joke in the world. I laugh too.

"I guess that makes me an asshole," he says, still laughing.

"No! You're an exception."

"Thank you."

"How do you do it?" I ask.

He shrugs. "I guess it just comes natural. Hey! That's Pam!"

A small SUV pulls into the lot. Dave waves. She pulls up alongside us and rolls down her window. Pam is blond, about thirty years old, with frown lines framing her thin lips.

"Sorry I'm late, DQ," she says, making it sound as if she is not sorry at all.

"No problem," Dave says. "God, you are beautiful!"

She rolls her eyes and pops the tailgate. Dave throws his bag in back. She is looking at me with a weary, puzzled expression. I don't know if I should introduce myself or what.

"Pam, this is my friend Stiggy. I told him we could give him a lift."

Pam is clearly not pleased. "Lift to where?"

"Perfect Village. He has to pick up his car."

"And I have to get back to work."

"It's cool, Pam. It's almost on the way." He's giving his smile everything he's got.

Pam tries to hold it back, but she gives up and grins back at him. "You are so full of it, DQ. Prairie Village is the other way."

He grins. "You know I got no sense of direction."

"You've got no sense of any kind." Still smiling.

I say, "It's okay. I don't want to inconvenience you."

"Don't be ridiculous," she says. "Hop in."

Dave walks around to the passenger door; I get in back, and she takes off.

"How's Trent?" she asks.

"He's doing great! I mean, considering he's in jail. Seems happy enough."

Pam shakes her head. "You Quigleys, I swear to God. You'd call tornado weather a beautiful day."

Dave laughs and turns to look at me. "Do you have an address?"

I dig out the cell phone bill and read off Bran's address.

"You know where that is?" Dave asks Pam.

"No, but my phone does." She thumbs the address into her phone, driving with one hand on the wheel and one eye on the road. "Fourteen minutes," she says, and speeds up.

I spend the next fourteen minutes in a mental loop. Dave and Pam are talking, but I'm not listening. I'm wondering what the chances are that Bran—and my car—are actually going to be there. He could be anywhere in the country. And if he's not there, then what? Walk back to the bus station? Hitch a ride and hope I don't get picked up by another pair of meth heads? And hitch a ride to where? Right now, *I have no destination* sounds pretty damn unappealing.

We enter Prairie Village, and I can see right away how it got its nickname. It's a suburb of curving streets, gentle hills, and immaculate houses with immaculate yards. The maples on every block are blazing red and orange like they've been programmed for fall, and the shrubbery is trimmed with cartoonish precision. It's one of those almost-wealthy neighborhoods— not mansion and chauffeured-limousine rich, but a lot richer than where I grew up. It figures that Bran would come from a place like this.

We come to one of those homes that are designed to look older than they are, with fake-weathered brick front, a red tile roof, and a circular driveway.

"This the place?" Pam says.

I can see the Mustang from the street, parked under an arbor next to the garage, and my heart almost explodes.

"Yes!"

My car! Where I thought it would be! I claw at the door handle. Dave throws an arm over the seat and grabs my shoulder.

"Easy," he says. "Wait for us to stop."

"That's my car!" I exclaim.

"Cool. Just be cool."

Pam brings her car to a stop a few yards past the driveway. Dave shifts around in his seat and gives me an uncharacteristically somber look.

"This dude stole your car, right?"

I nod.

"You got another set of keys?"

I don't.

"So, what are you gonna do?"

"Knock on the door?"

"You want me to go with you?"

"D!" Pam jabs him with her elbow. "I have to get back to work!"

"I'll be fine," I say as I shoulder open the door. I'm not sure that's true, but I don't want Dave's smile to get my car back. I don't want there to be any smiling.

"You sure?"

"Yeah." I step out. "Thanks for the ride."

"No problem!" Dave gives me one last grin for the road. I close the car door, and they drive off. I walk across the perfect lawn to my car. Maybe he left the key in it. Nope, the doors are locked. I peer through the driver's side window. Except for a couple of crumpled McDonald's bags on the passenger seat, it looks okay. But I need my keys.

I cross the cobblestone driveway. The front door is massive. It looks as if it has been hammered by a thousand workers with tiny hammers, then painted over—fake antique. A brass door knocker is affixed to the door at head height, but it's fake too. It takes me a minute to find the doorbell, which turns out to be a button on the fake door knocker. I press it and hear, faintly, a series of chimes from inside the house.

It takes approximately forever. I look up and see a beige plastic box mounted above the lintel. Security camera. The door opens. A woman looks out at me. She has a face like a marble statue and a helmet of platinum blond hair that looks as if it would crack under pressure.

"Can I help you?" she says.

I haven't rehearsed what I'll say. What comes out sounds like a croak.

"That's my car," I say, pointing toward the Mustang. She doesn't exactly roll her eyes, but her lack of

expression conveys as much. She closes the door part-
way and calls out.

"Brandon! One of your friends is here." She leaves
the door slightly ajar. Not open enough to imply an
invitation to come in, so I stay where I am. After
another minute the door opens wide.

I almost don't recognize him. Bran's hair is now
short, clean, and brushed back from his forehead. He
is wearing clean jeans and a white polo shirt almost
identical to mine, except his is newer and whiter.
Instead of a penguin embroidered on the left chest,
his has a little red-and-blue KU.

His eyes widen when he sees me, but it only lasts a
moment before he recovers his blasé face.

"Oh," he says. "You. What do you want?"

"What do you think? You stole my car!" My fists are
bunched hard, and I'm shaking.

He shrugs and sniffs. "I just borrowed it, dude. Don't
get all drama queen. I don't want your crappy car."

"Give me my keys!"

"All right, all right. Just hang on." He backs away and
disappears. I step inside. The entrance foyer is enormous. An elaborate chandelier hangs from the twenty-
foot-high ceiling. Bran is ascending a curving, carpeted
staircase. The woman—his mother, I assume—is posed
with her arms crossed in front of a side table. On the
table is the life-size armless torso of a goddess. A plas-
ter copy of some Roman relic, I think. The woman and
the goddess look like they could be related.

"Your son stole my car," I say.

Her mouth tightens slightly. "Brandon *borrowed* your car," she says, as if correcting a grammatical error.

"Yeah, right. Without permission. Then drove it three hundred miles away."

No reaction. A few seconds later Bran comes padding down the stairs. He is barefoot. A set of keys dangles from his forefinger. When he reaches the bottom step, he flicks his wrist and the keys come flying toward me. I catch them, barely.

"You're a real asshole, you know that?" I say.

Bran smiles and shrugs one shoulder.

"I think you should leave now," his mother says.

I look at the keys. Car key, house key, and a key to my bike lock. No reason to stay, but I'm mad, and I want some acknowledgment that I've been wronged.

"He owes me money," I say to his mother.

"I didn't take your money!" Bran says.

"You took my car. I had to come all the way across Missouri to find it. You owe me—" I don't know what he owes me. "You owe me bus fare at least! And for my time."

Bran's mother makes a *pfft* sound with her lips and lifts her purse from the table behind her. She opens her wallet, extracts a bill, and hands it to Bran.

"Give this to the boy, Brandon," she says.

Bran twists his face into a pained expression, then crosses the foyer and thrusts the bill at me. It's a hundred dollars. More than I expected, since I didn't think I'd get anything.

"Thanks, *Cake*," I say.

The startled expression on his face almost makes it worth it.

# Dreams

**Getting rid of all my Darth Vaders—and Garf**
along with them, I guess—felt like tearing off a scab.
It hurt, but in a way I was relieved. It was as if I'd
moved on to the next thing, whatever that was.

Mom was sitting in the kitchen in her Zumba outfit
with a cup of herbal tea, staring into space the way she
did a lot. She barely acknowledged me when I walked
past her and grabbed a carton of orange juice from
the fridge. I guess I didn't acknowledge her, either.
We'd been ignoring each other a lot lately. I drank the
juice straight from the carton. Usually she would yell
at me for doing that, but she didn't. She did look at
me, though.

"How was school?" she asked, pretending to care.

I shrugged. "Same old."

She nodded. I went to my room and looked at the empty shelves. I counted the money in my wallet. I called Gaia's number and listened to the voice telling me that the number was no longer in service. I looked at the blister on my heel. The loose skin had rubbed off from walking to Brain Food, and there was just a weeping red circle the size of a quarter. I got some ointment from the bathroom cabinet and smeared it on and put on a Band-Aid that didn't quite cover it. I turned on my computer and searched for Prairie du Chien on Google Maps. Turns out it's a small town on the Wisconsin side of the Mississippi, a couple hundred miles southeast of Saint Andrew Valley. I clicked on satellite view, zoomed down to street level and cruised around town. I saw frozen images of people walking, driving, sitting. None of them were Gaia. Of course not—those photos had been shot in the spring. I could tell from the lilacs blooming. Gaia and I had just been getting to know each other back then. Besides, what if I *had* seen her? She didn't want anything to do with me.

I flopped down on my bed and put my pillow over my face, wrapped my arms around it, and squeezed it over my ears so I couldn't see or hear, wishing there was something I could do to shut down what I was feeling. A drug, maybe, like a huge shot of novocaine that would make my body and mind completely numb. Was that how drug addicts got started?

Something bad happened, and all they wanted was to shut it down? Was that what had made my dad shoot himself in the neck on a park bench all alone? What if it was genetic?

No. My grandparents—the three I had left—had all made it into their eighties, and so far as I knew, none of them were suicidal. Although, Grandma Teresa— my dad's mom—was kind of cranky. I couldn't blame her. She lived in a senior living place up in Saint Cloud with a bunch of other cranky old people.

Why was I thinking about Grandma Teresa? I squeezed the pillow harder, so hard I could feel my skull pressing in on my brain, and I saw Garf's new shoes swinging from that wire. I blocked that out and thought about Gaia alone in the caves with a dead flashlight, feeling her way along the rough sandstone walls.

I couldn't breathe. Was it possible to smother yourself? I'd probably just pass out.

I let go. I could see the impression of my face on the pillow, the dent where my nose had been and two wet spots from my eyes. I'd been crying and I hadn't even known it. I threw the pillow aside and stared up at the cracks in the ceiling, more familiar to me than my own face. I waited for the next god-awful thought to descend upon me. Something inside my abdomen stirred, a new sensation. Hunger! Yes! I could do something about that! I turned my head and looked at the clock. Seven-forty-six? How had it gotten so late?

Out in the hallway it was dark, but I could see a bar of light beneath Mom's bedroom door. I went to the kitchen. The sink was full of dishes, and there was one place setting at the table with a chicken breast, some fried potatoes, and a cucumber salad on the plate. Why hadn't she called me for dinner? Maybe she had, and I hadn't heard her because I'd had the pillow wrapped around my head.

I ate the cold chicken and the cold potatoes and the salad, then found a bag of chips in the cupboard and crunched on those until they were gone. When I stopped chewing, the silence was sudden and complete. What was my mom doing? I went to her bedroom door and listened. After a minute of hearing nothing, I knocked.

"Mom?"

"What?" Her voice sounded normal. Some of the tension went out of me. I didn't want to think about what I'd been thinking.

"Nothing," I said. "I just wasn't sure you were home."

"I'm reading."

Of course she was reading. She read all the time. But usually she read in her chair in the living room, not in bed with her door closed.

"Okay," I said.

I washed the dishes, a task I usually hated, but on that night I welcomed the mindlessness of it: wash, rinse, dry, repeat. When I'd finished, I went out to the garage and sat in Dad's car, hands on the wheel, eyes closed, imagining a road, any road. I saw the land-scape flashing by, and something on the horizon. A mountain? Clouds? Smoke? What was the last thing my dad saw? The river? The trees? The sky?

I fell asleep and dreamed about driving, and I didn't wake up until the morning light flooded in through the garage door's frosted-glass windows.

# "Rumble"

## Kelis
## 3:35

**My car reeks of cigarettes and fast food. I** toss the crumpled McDonald's bags onto Bran's lawn. He was using the McDonald's cup for an ashtray; it's a quarter full of melted ice and cigarette butts and ashes. I throw that out too.

I start the car. The gas tank is near empty. I put the car in reverse and look over my shoulder to back out, and I see Bran standing there. He waves and comes up to my open window.

"Hey," he says.

"What do you want?"

"Just wanted to say I'm sorry about borrowing your car, is all."

"You left me with an empty tank."

"Sorry. Tell you what, can you give me a ride?"

I can't believe this guy. He steals my car, and then he asks me for a ride?

I force out a laugh. "Get lost."

I start backing out. He walks along beside the car.

"I just need a lift over to Brookside." He looks back at the house. "I gotta get out of here. My mom's being a total bitch."

"Gee, I wonder why?"

"Ouch! Tell you what, I'll buy you a tank of gas."

A tank of gas? I could use that. And I'm curious. This version of Bran is like a different person. I might not have recognized him if I'd passed him on the street.

"Okay, get in," I say.

"Thanks!" He runs around to the passenger side and gets in. "She wants me to go back to school and be a doctor or lawyer or some shit. Like she never heard of a gap year? I want to go to Europe, man. Someplace fun."

"Where's the nearest gas station?" I ask.

Bran points; I follow his directions. "School's for losers. I went to KU for two semesters. Everybody I met there was some sort of asshole." He pulls out a pack of Marlboros. "Mind if I smoke?"

"Yes."

He sighs theatrically and puts away his cigs. "What a sucky summer," he says.

"It's fall."

"That Allie, what a stone-cold frigid bitch she

turned out to be. Can you believe her with that stinky Rasta Randy? Turn left up here."

I turn left.

"People suck, man. Here, the QuikTrip on the corner."

I pull into the QuikTrip and stop at a pump.

"I can't believe I hung with those two for so long," he says. "Allie waving those tits at me twenty-four seven."

"You going to pay for gas or what?" I say.

"Yeah, yeah, relax. I'll buy your gas." He gets out and swipes a credit card—probably his mom's—at the pump. I pop open the gas tank door. He says, "I suppose you want me to pump it too."

I get out and put the pump nozzle in the gas tank.

"I hear you tried to rape her," I say as the pump chugs away.

"Who? Allie? That what she said? What a bitch. She was coming on to me, man! I try to join her in her little tent, and she goes apeshit on me. And that phony Rasta, Randy, he's all, like, macho man all of a sudden. Like he's saving her virtue. *Virtue?* Shit, she'd do it with anybody."

"But not you?"

"Not you either. I'm going inside and grab a Coke."

Bran goes into the store. The pump clicks off. I pull the nozzle out of the tank and twist on the gas cap. I get behind the wheel and start the car.

A few seconds later Bran comes out of the store looking pissed off. He gets in and says, "Asshole won't let me put a Coke on my credit card. Minimum purchase, my ass. I just bought you a tank of gas! I swear to God, my whole life is nothing but one asshole after another."

I stare at him, at his fresh haircut and shave, at his clean polo shirt with the KU logo embroidered on the chest, at his mom's credit card still clutched in his hand. It's like looking in a distorted mirror.

"Get out," I say.

He looks at me, startled.

"Get out," I repeat.

"What the hell? Dude, I just gassed you up!"

"Get out."

"Screw that! We had a deal. Let's go."

He must see something in my face, because he shoulders open the door and climbs out, all the while yelling every profanity I know, and then some. He slams the door so hard, my ears pop.

He's still screaming at me as I pull away.

# "No One Knows"

## Queens of the Stone Age
## 4:39

**Leaving Bran stranded at the QuikTrip feels** fantastic. Payback! I showed him! I won! I'm free, while he's stuck with being Brandon Fetzig in Perfect Village, and I got my car back. I can be anybody I want to be. I can go anywhere.

If I can find my way out of this tangled mess of suburban streets.

I pull over at a Starbucks and use their Wi-Fi to check my iPod. Turns out I'm just half a mile south of I-70, the freeway I took across Missouri. Now I know where I am, but I have another problem. I don't know where I'm going. Maybe it doesn't matter.

I head north to the freeway and head east toward the Great River Road, on the other side of the state.

A destination! When I get there, I'll decide which way to go.

The good feeling fades even before I get out of the city. Thinking about Bran gets me to thinking about Garf Neff, about something I said to him, that I thought I was an asshole magnet. Bran was saying almost exactly the same thing only in different words, and he's an asshole with a capital A. So what does that make me?

Then I remember something Allie said that night in the canoe.

It hits me like a punch to the gut, as if an invisible airbag had exploded and slammed into my belly. I veer left, across the other lane and onto the shoulder, trying to breathe. A semi roars by, horn blasting. I take a shuddering breath, check my mirror, speed up, and pull back onto the roadway. I'm shaking.

She said I was a lot like Bran. I thought she was just teasing, but now I'm not so sure. A lot of the other stuff she said made a lot of sense.

Am I really like Bran? Does being an asshole magnet make me the asshole?

Am I going back home to my mom, like Bran? Back to my suburban life with clean shirts and school five days a week? Is that where I'm headed? What will happen if I do? I don't know if I can, and that scares me. What if I go back, and Mom tells me to get lost?

I've hardly thought about my mom at all since I left home, and now when I think about her, it's

two-dimensional, like panels in a comic book. I have
this thing. It's called a mom. She eats, sleeps, goes to
work, goes to yoga, goes to Zumba, and yells at me. She
doesn't really yell, not literally. She just complains. I
guess she has a lot to complain about. Does she miss
me? I don't know. I'm sure she's mad at me. She canceled the credit card. If I go home . . . what will I find?
Open arms? Crossed arms? I mean, I stole her credit
card and didn't tell her where I was going. I haven't
called. Is she going out of her mind with worry? Or is
she relieved that I left? One less problem to deal with.
One less mouth to feed.

Another semi roars by on my left. I look at the
speedometer. I'm only going forty-five miles per hour.
I speed up. I turn on the music. A song by Queens of
the Stone Age comes on. I crank it up until it shat-
ters all the thoughts in my brain. I blow past Odessa,
Concordia, and Sweet Springs. I listen to my father's
music, marveling at the man I never knew. The Clash,
Eminem, Motörhead, Marilyn Manson—a string of
angries. How did I not know this about Dad, about
his music? Marshall Junction, Chouteau Springs,
Windsor Place—I see the exit signs, but the towns are
invisible from the freeway. Columbia is coming up. I
see a broken-down Ford on the shoulder. It looks like it
used to be a cop car. It looks like Honeypie and Babe's
car. Maybe somebody stole it out of that Walmart parking lot and it broke down. I drive through Columbia
without stopping.

When I left Saint Andrew Valley, I was looking forward to mindless hours of watching fence posts flash by, but it turns out there is no such thing as mindless. Even with music pounding at my ears—Nirvana, Pink Floyd—I'm still thinking about stuff. I suspect that even sleep won't turn off the thinking. I could be in a coma, and my thoughts would continue to churn, slowly, those little electrical impulses firing as long as my heart is beating. Was that what made Dad do it? Was dying the only way to make it stop?

I don't want to die. But I wouldn't mind being dead for a while. Eastville, Kingdom City, Danville. I exit the freeway and turn north to avoid Saint Louis. It's better on the smaller roads. More things to see, decisions to make, cars and animals and people to avoid. The music changes. Somebody I never heard of named Peggy Lee is singing about fires and rejection and circuses and death, then Regina Spektor, who I have heard of, singing about her broken heart, then Suzanne Vega singing about a kid whose parents are beating the crap out of him, and my cheeks are wet because it's so sad to think that there are people who have shittier lives than me. Then a Beatles song comes on, and it's so cheerful and sunny, I can't stand it, so I shut off the stereo and drive.

After another half hour I turn east. Sooner or later I'll hit the river. I imagine driving right into it, imagine the car plowing nose-first into the sluggish, muddy waters, then sinking. They say it's impossible to open the doors because of the water pressure. You have to roll down a window and let the water in and hold your breath until the car is almost full, then open the door. The Mustang has electric windows. Would they work if the car was sitting at the bottom of a river? Am I strong enough to break the window with my fist? I remember the guy at the Foodland punching the window. He was bigger than me, and he couldn't break it.

It doesn't matter. I know I'm not driving into any river. I just like to imagine it: one scary moment when I am not thinking about Gaia or my mom or my dad or what I'm going to do next.

# Superman

**When I was six, I thought my dad was like** Superman—infinitely strong, invulnerable, and knowing everything there was to know. He could pick me up with one arm, answer any question, shrug off any injury. It wouldn't have surprised me if he'd been able to fly, or if bullets had bounced off his chest. I guess that's how a lot of six-year-olds look at their dads.

I wanted to be Superman too. I'd tie a red beach towel around my neck to make a cape and fly around the house in my underwear with my arms thrust out in front of me. One time my dad came out of the bathroom, and I charged at him and, with every ounce of my forty-eight pounds, rammed both fists into his belly. Well, maybe it was a few inches below that. I wasn't that tall.

I expected to bounce off and fall to the floor giggling, but I didn't. He fell to the floor, gasping, his face contorted with pain. It scared me. I'd never seen him like that before, never known that I could hurt him, never known that anything could hurt him.

"I'm sorry!" I said. He tried to laugh it off, but his face was all twisted, and it took him a minute to get up. He walked all hunched over into the living room and lowered himself to the sofa.

"I'll be okay, Stevie," he said.

I think it was a first for him, too. I don't think he knew until that moment that I could hurt him.

# "Highway 61 Revisited"

## Bob Dylan
## 3:30

**I choose roads semi-randomly, moving in** a generally easterly direction, dodging thoughts of guilt and grieving and loneliness. I become a connoisseur of barns. The best barns are big and a bit crooked, weathered but still in use, with a cupola up top and fading ads painted on the sides. I do not like the ones painted colors other than red, or with metal sides, or with holes in the roof.

One of those barns—one of the good ones—has a side covered with an old tobacco advertisement, barely readable. I slow down for a closer look. I can make out some of the letters:

A R K T W A

CIGARS

ARK TWA Cigars?

Oh, I get it. "MARK TWAIN," with the outside letters worn off. I must be getting close to Hannibal.

I come up over a low rise and see a billboard: WORLD-FAMOUS MARK TWAIN CAVE.

Definitely Hannibal. I don't want to go back to Hannibal. Been there, done that. I turn north on the next road I come to—a dirt track that might not even be a road. Could just be a long driveway—brown cornstalks on my left, a fallow field on my right. After a mile I decide it's a road, so I keep going. Eventually I hit US Highway 61, the same Highway 61 that goes from Minnesota all the way to Louisiana. There's a Bob Dylan song about it on the iPod. It's a divided highway with not much traffic. I turn left, the direction Hannibal isn't. That means I'm going north, toward Minnesota.

Am I going home? I still don't know.

Almost immediately I see a billboard for the Mark Twain Casino and RV Park, and I wonder if I turned the wrong way. But the Mark Twain Casino is in a place called La Grange. I keep going. At the La Grange exit I pass a hitchhiker. I drive past him, go about a quarter mile, then pull over and back down the shoulder until he sees me. He waves and runs to meet me. I stop the car; he opens the door.

"Dude!" he says. "I thought that was you!"

"Hey, Knob," I say.

# Hahn/Cock

**I had to take a running start. It took me three** tries before I made it up the steep side of the metal pyramid. I grabbed one of the big blue chicken legs and pulled myself onto the flat top. The bright blue rooster towered above me. I stood up and rested my hand on the chicken's wing and looked out over the sculpture garden.

That was a week after Gaia left, when I'd been torturing myself by going to all the places we used to go.

"Now?" asked the girl standing below me holding my phone. I didn't know her, but she had agreed to take my picture.

"Wait," I said.

"It looks even bigger with you up there," she said.

"Just wait." I circled the chicken, looking for hand-holds. One of the tail feathers was within reach. I gripped it with both hands and pulled myself up onto the chicken's back, and straddled it like a rider. From the top of the chicken I looked out over the sculpture garden. I could see the freeway, the Basilica, and behind me the Walker Art Center. Two guards came out of the doors and started running toward us. I waved at the two girls.

"Okay!" I shouted.

The girl with my phone took a picture. She moved to the side for a different angle and shot me again.

"Got it!" she yelled.

I slid off the rooster's back, then down the side of the pyramid. The guards were fifty yards away. I grabbed my phone from the girl, yelled, "Thanks!" and took off running.

When I got home, I texted the photos to Gaia's number. She wouldn't see them, of course. None of my texts were going through. But I sent them anyway.

# "Yon Yonson"

## Traditional folk song

**Bob the Knob is wearing the same clothes he** had on the first time I picked him up, and he doesn't smell any better. I crack my window and ease back onto the highway.

"Did your farm job not work out?" I ask him.

He shrugs. "It was okay. Didn't last, though." He shows me his gap-toothed grin. "Had a little altercation with the boss. So I guess, for ol' Knob, it's back to the lab again."

"Lab?"

"Just an expression. I got folk up in Wisconsin, maybe find work at one of the mills up there. Maybe get some dental, get my choppers fixed." He grins. "It's all good."

"How so?"

"Things work out, is all. Always have. I been blessed."

Knob does not strike me as a man who has been blessed. He could use a shower, a change of clothes, and a new canine tooth—in that order.

"So where you headed this round?" he asks.

"I haven't decided."

"You got to find your people, dude," he says. "Folks down in Hannibal, those weren't my people." He draws a breath and sings:

> My name is Yon Yonson,
> I live in Wisconsin,
> I work in da lumber mill dere.
> I walk down da street,
> And da people I meet,
> Say, "Hey, what's your name?"
> and I say,
> "My name is Yon Yonson,
> I live in—"

Knob breaks into a coughing fit, thankfully ending the song.

"Born and raised," Knob says when he's done coughing. "A man's got to know who he is." He gives me an intent look. "You know who you are?"

"Yeah, you told me last time. I'm a *nexus*."

"Oh. I guess I did." He sits back. "Anyways, it's true."

We ride in silence for a time. Every so often he shifts around, trying to get comfortable, and a waft of funk comes off him. I roll my window down a bit more and wonder why I picked him up. I suppose because he was a familiar face.

"You got a gal?" he asks. People keep asking me that. I wish they would stop.

"Not anymore."

"She give you the heave-ho, huh? Been there. What'd you do to piss her off?"

"I don't know."

"You best find out, dude, or the next one's gonna dump you too."

*Next one?*

He says, "Nothing happens but what there's a reason for it. Like, you picking me up both coming and going. You think that's a coincidence?"

"I don't know what else it could be."

"Me neither, but it's damn sure something."

"You don't believe in coincidences?"

"Sure, I do. But I don't believe they're coincidental, know what I mean?"

"No."

"Just seems like coincidences come at the oddest times."

I didn't think Gaia dumping me was a coincidence, but Knob was right about one thing. There was a reason for it.

And I had no idea what it was.

Highway 61 takes us past Alexandria, across the Des Moines River, and into Iowa. I'm not seeing dead possums anymore, just raccoons. It's getting late. By the time we pass Keokuk, the sun has set. We don't talk much. Knob stares vacantly out the side window. I watch the road.

"You planning to drive all night?" Knob asks after a long silence.

I shrug. I really don't know. I'm not tired.

"Don't suppose you're going anywhere near Rhine-lander," he says.

"I don't know where that is."

"A good bit north."

"I'm going to Prairie du Chien," I hear myself say. *When did I decide that*?

"Prairie, huh? I been there a bunch a times. What's in Prairie?"

"My girlfriend," I say.

"The one dumped you?"

"You said I should find out why."

"I did?" He snorts. "I say all kinds of stuff." He puts his seat back and wriggles down until his knees press against the glove box. "We got about a four-hour drive. Mind I catch a little shuteye?"

"Knock yourself out," I say.

Knob snores. Not a steady, soothing snore, but a series of wheezy stops and snorting starts. I think maybe he has sleep apnea. My dad had sleep apnea. Mom was always complaining about it and trying to get him to see a doctor, but he never did. Maybe he figured he was going to kill himself anyway, so what did it matter?

Knob is nothing like my dad. For one thing, my dad smelled a lot better.

I stop at a gas station in Dubuque. Knob doesn't wake up. I fill the tank, buy a couple of Red Bulls, and continue on Highway 61 through Dubuque, across the river, and into Wisconsin. We're going through a small town called Dickeyville when Knob snorts, spasms, and sits up.

"Where are we?" he asks in a sleep-guttered croak.

"Dickeyville," I tell him.

"I been there. Don't stop."

I hand him one of the Red Bulls. He pops the top and guzzles it.

"Hoo-*ee!*" he says. "Rhinelander, here I come!"

"I'm only going to Prairie du Chien," I remind him.

"No matter." He finishes off his Red Bull and crumples the can. "Can't get there from here anyways."

"Why not?"

"You ever hear of Zeno?"

"What's that?"

"This dead Greek dude. Philosopher. He proved you can't get anywhere, 'cause first you got to get halfways."

"Is this like that nexus thing?" I ask.

"What? No, man. This is, like, quantum. You want to get from A to B, first you've got to get halfway. And to get halfway, you have to get halfway to halfway. And to get to halfway to halfway, you got to get halfway to halfway to halfway."

"So?"

"So it keeps going to infinity, so to get anywhere at all it takes eternity. Can't be done."

"You're saying we're basically immobile?"

"Yeah. Except we move. But that's all perception. We just *think* we're moving."

"Where do you get this stuff?"

"I read books."

"If we just think we're moving, what's the point?"

"Good question. Maybe Zeno knew."

"Too bad he's dead."

"It's a goddamn Greek tragedy, is what it is."

Knob starts talking about a bunch of other philosophers. I'm pretty sure he's making most of it up. For example, I'm pretty sure Zorba the Greek was never a real person. I tune him out because I'm too tired to sort out which parts of what he's saying are true and which parts are BS. I figure it's mostly the latter.

I tune back in when Knob starts talking about his ex-wife. It surprises me because he doesn't seem like a guy who would ever have been married.

"Married five years before she up and dumped me," he says.

"What was her name?" I ask.

"I called her Booboo. Booboo and Knob." He laughs. "We had us some times, me and Booboo. She finally got sick of me being mostly between jobs and took up

with a fella from Milwaukee. Maybe that's what happened with your girl."

"I don't think so," I say, but I don't know.

By the time we reach Prairie du Chien, it's two in the
morning and Knob is snoring again. The gas tank is
low, so I pull into a BP. I'm not sure what to do with
Knob. I'd like to find a place to park and catch a few
hours of sleep, but not with him sitting next to me
snoring.

Knob solves that by waking up while I'm filling
the tank. He gets out of the car, stretches, and looks
around.

"We in Prairie?"

"Yeah."

He grabs his pack from the backseat.

"Thanks for the ride, man."

"How are you going to get to Rhinelander?" I ask.

"Same way I got here, I guess. Might hang out in
Prairie for a bit, though. Use to know some folk here."

"You take care."

"You too, man. Find that gal." He slings the pack
over his shoulder and walks off down the road as if he
knows exactly where he's going, even if you can't get
there from here.

# "Slack"

## NNB
## 4:04

**I wake up and smell Knob. I open my eyes.** It's light out. I turn my head. The passenger seat is empty; all that's left of Knob is his odor. Or maybe it's me. It's probably me.

I'm parked behind a warehouse. I remember pulling in last night, barely able to stay awake. Mine is the only car in the lot. I check my iPod. Six a.m. Saturday. I start the car and roll down the window. It's chilly, but the fresh air is welcome. I'm glad I didn't give Bran back his hoodie. I drive down main street, Marquette Road, until I see a McDonald's. I buy an Egg McMuffin and a Coke and eat in one of the booths so I can use their Wi-Fi to search for Maeve Samms.

I find her on Facebook right away. But we're not

Facebook friends, so there is no contact information and I can't see her posts. I can see her photos, though. There are a lot of them. Mostly animal pictures: cats, cows, horses, dogs, chickens. Some of the shots are from school back in Saint Andrew Valley. Selfies with her friends. I scroll through until I find one with Gaia in it, looking right at me. I spread the image until her face fills the screen, and I draw a shaky breath. It's an old picture, probably taken back when I first met her.

I keep scrolling and find a couple of recent pictures of Gaia. In one she is standing in front of an enormous hairy bull, grinning. No makeup. Her hair is shorter, barely brushing the shoulders of her flannel shirt. The other picture is with Maeve, their cheeks pressed together, sticking out their tongues. At me, I imagine.

I go through the photos one by one, looking for clues as to where they might be. I know it's a farm near Prairie du Chien, but that's all. Finally I find something. A picture of a wrought iron arch, a gate decorated with metal leaves and shocks of wheat. At the top of the arch, fashioned from welded metal, are the words "Prairie Haven."

I Google "Prairie Haven" and find several places by that name: an antiques store, a town in Kansas, a motel, and a nudist resort. Nothing near Prairie du Chien. I go back to Maeve's Facebook page and look at the pictures of Gaia again. It's like looking through a window into another world, a different reality. For a moment I think maybe she can feel me looking at her, but the moment passes. I go to the restroom and wash my face and clean my teeth with my finger and a piece of paper towel. I have a toothbrush, but it's in my bag; I'll have to do a better job later.

I stop at the counter on the way out. The girl who sold me the Egg McMuffin looks about my age. I order an apple pie and ask her if she knows Maeve Samms. She doesn't. I ask her if she's ever heard of a farm called Prairie Haven. She hasn't. I ask her where the high school is. She points and says, "It's just a couple blocks that way."

I drive over to the school—Prairie du Chien High School, "Home of the Blackhawks." It's a big brick building surrounded by athletic fields. No one is around. Of course not. Duh. It's Saturday.

Not sure what to do next, I drive around looking for ideas. Just outside town I see a place called Tractor Supply Company. I pull in and ask the guy behind the counter if he knows Prairie Haven, or a farmer named Samms. He doesn't. I go back downtown. Where would Gaia and Maeve hang out? They couldn't stay on the farm all the time. I park in an area with a bunch of businesses—sporting goods, barber shop, insurance company, boutiques, and a funny little square building, not much bigger than a garden shed, plunked down in the middle of a parking lot full of boats. The name PETE'S is painted on the awning. Pete's *what*? No clue. Whatever it is, it's not open.

I continue down the sidewalk and come to a coffee

shop. I go inside. It's perfect. Coffee, tea, smoothies, soup, and sandwiches. It smells great. If Gaia was within fifty miles of this place, she'd come here. I wish I hadn't eaten at McDonald's.

There are a dozen people at the tables. None of them are Gaia. I order a cappuccino. The guy at the counter is about forty. I ask him if he knows Maeve Samms or Gaia Nygren.

"Are they customers?" he asks.

"I think so."

"What do they look like?"

"Um . . . they're my age? Maeve is blond, sort of thin with long hair?"

He chuckles. "That could be half the girls in Prairie."

"Gaia has dark hair."

"That'd be the other half." He laughs, then turns and calls to the barista, "Hey, Naomi, you know a couple of girls named Maeve and Gaia?"

"I think I've written 'Maeve' on a few cups," she says. She has short hair, almost like you can see her scalp on the sides, and a ring in her right nostril. "But I don't know her."

While I'm waiting at the end of the counter for my coffee, I log on to Facebook and find Maeve's photos. When the barista slides my cappuccino to me, I notice a tiny tattoo on her wrist, a plus sign with a circle around it. I show her the picture of Maeve and Gaia sticking out their tongues.

"I've seen them in here," she says, and points at

Gaia. "This one always orders a mango smoothie."

*Score!*

"Are they here a lot?"

"Pretty often." She gives me a doubtful look, as if she's thinking she told me too much. "Are they friends of yours?"

"Yeah. From school."

She nods, lips pressed tight together, and starts to fill another order.

I take my cappuccino to a table where I can watch the front door and wait. It is possible to make a cappuccino last for an hour. I make mine last two. People come and go. None of them are Maeve. None of them are Gaia. I use the time to rehearse what I'll say to Gaia.

Starting with, *Hello*. No, wait. *Hey!* That's more casual. Or, *Oh! Hi!* Like I just happened to be there and I'm surprised to see her. Or maybe just a cool look, lift one eyebrow and wait for her to come over to me. She'd have to, right? She couldn't just ignore me. I don't think. Could she?

What about the big romantic gesture? Rush into her open arms and lift her up and kiss her, like in the movies? I know she watches those movies, but I think in real life she might just clobber me. Maybe I should do nothing and wait to see what she does. I imagine her opening the door and stepping into the coffee shop. It's a bright, sunny day, so she might stop inside the door to let her eyes adjust. Would she see me right away? I'm sitting toward the back, so she might not. Maybe she'll be with Maeve, and Maeve will spot me and grab Gaia's arm and point. Or she might be with someone else. What if she's with a guy? If that happens, I'll play it cool, like I don't really care even though thinking about it now is like having a chain saw ripping my guts open from the inside out.

My thoughts are interrupted by the barista, Naomi, who is walking around with a rag wiping down the tabletops.

"So, are you a stalker?" she asks.

"Me? No! Why?" I'm confused.

"You're looking for those two girls, showing their picture."

"Oh. No. One of them is . . . I used to go out with her before she moved here, and I was just passing through and thought maybe I'd look her up."

"The mango smoothie?"

"Yeah. With the long black hair. Except on Facebook it looks like she cut it."

"I get that," Naomi says. "I used to have long hair too, but I got sick of it, so"—she shrugs and gestures at her buzz cut—"*c'est la vie.*"

"It looks good," I say, and on her it does.

"Thanks. Actually, the reason I cut it is because my boyfriend broke up with me." She laughs. "Kind of a cliché, I know, but whatever."

"Maybe I should get a haircut."

"She dumped you, huh?"

"Well, she moved."

"Are you sure you're not stalking her?"

"Yes! I mean, no, I'm not."

She gives me a long look, like she's making a decision; then she nods and looks at my cup. Nothing left but a few flecks of drying foam. "You want me to take that for you?"

"Thanks."

"You want another one?"

I don't, but I say yes, because if I have a cup in front of me, I figure I can keep sitting there. A couple minutes later she brings me a fresh cappuccino. I reach for my wallet, but Naomi waves it away.

"On the house," she says. "But you've got to promise me something. If your girlfriend comes in and says she wants you to leave her alone, you listen to her. Okay?"

When I think about stalking, I think about this creepy kid from Fairview, the town right next to Saint Andrew Valley, who was obsessed with this girl, and he got caught climbing up a tree at night so he could watch her through her bedroom window. I heard he was always staring at her in school, too. I never met the kid, but I guess everybody hated him. Anyway, he finally set his parents' house on fire and ended up in some mental hospital.

That's not me. I'm not climbing trees or skulking in the shadows. I just want to talk to her. Knob was kind of a knob head, but he was right about one thing: everything happens for a reason. I want to know why she moved, and why she blocked me from her phone. I *need* to know. I am not a stalker.

I make the second cappuccino last until I can't stand to sit there any longer. Naomi watches me put my cup in the dish tray.

"You leaving?" she asks.

I nod.

"If your girlfriend shows up, do you want me to tell her you're looking for her?"

"Sure."

"What's your name?"

"Steven? Steve. Stiggy."

She laughs. "That's a lot of names!"

"Stiggy," I say.

"Okay, Stiggy. Got it."

Outside, the weather has warmed up. It's one of those bright October days in the midseventies. I'm planning to walk around the neighborhood and check back at the coffee shop every so often. I turn right and immediately see a line of a couple dozen people on the sidewalk. They're lined up in front of Pete's, the little shack I noticed before. I walk over to see what's going on, and smell cooking. Hamburgers. I haven't eaten since McDonald's, and that was hours ago. My mouth starts watering. I get in line behind a family: mom, dad, and three boys, maybe five, six, and seven years old.

"What's the deal here?" I ask the dad. He's wearing a Minnesota Twins cap.

"Best burgers anywhere," he says. The line isn't moving. "We drive down from Winona just for a Pete's burger. You're lucky. This is their last weekend; then they close down until spring."

"What makes them so good?" I ask.

"They're just really special." He shrugs. "Also, it's a nice drive. Follow the river road all the way, and when we get here, we're all starving for a Pete's."

Several more people have lined up behind me, and the line hasn't moved an inch.

I say, "How long does it take to get to the window?"

"Not long. It comes in waves," the dad says. A minute after he says that, the line starts moving. The people at the front are leaving clutching wax paper sacks. Some of them go to their cars; some just start chowing down right there on the sidewalk. They look happy. We shuffle forward, and the line stops again.

The five-year-old is working up to having a tantrum. "I'm *huungreeee!*" he whines.

The second-oldest kid punches him in the shoulder; the little kid lets out a howl. The mom grabs both of them, the middle one by the ear and the little one by the collar. "Mind yourselves, or we turn around and go straight home."

"Not fair!" yells the oldest kid.

"Life isn't fair," the mom says. "Now behave!"

The dad chuckles and says to me, "Like I say, comes

in waves. Just like life. See these kids? Popped 'em out one after another. Piece a cake."

The mom narrows her eyes at him and says, "That how you see it, Herm?"

"I'm just talking, hon."

She sniffs and turns her back to us, still hanging on to the one kid's ear.

"What they do is cook a full griddle," the dad says. "Forty, fifty burgers at a time. Takes about ten minutes or so. Then they serve 'em up quick like. Next wave, it'll be our turn."

I look back down the street toward the coffee shop. No Gaia, but I see a ragged figure coming up the other side of the street. It's Knob. He slows and looks over at Pete's.

The line lurches forward, and the next thing I know, I'm standing at the window and an older woman is asking me for my order. I look back at Knob. He's still on the sidewalk, shuffling along.

"Two cheeseburgers," I say.

"No cheese."

I don't know what to say to that.

"With or without?" she asks.

"With or without what?"

"Onions."

"Okay, two no-cheese burgers, one with and one without."

"Ketchup or mustard?"

"Can I get both?"

"Sure, you can. Yellow or brown?"

"Yellow?" This is getting very complicated for a burger stand that doesn't even have cheese.

"Chips?"

"No, thanks."

"To drink?"

I look at the cans lined up on the shelf next to her.

"A Pepsi and a Mountain Dew."

Behind her a guy is standing at a huge, steaming griddle covered with blobs of meat and a pile of sliced onions swimming in a shallow lake of greasy water. It looks like the burgers are being boiled. He scoops up a dripping patty covered with onions, sticks it in a bun, and wraps it with wax paper. Thirty seconds later I'm running across the street to catch up with Knob.

"With or without?" I say.

Knob jumps like I've goosed him. He sees me and smiles, then sees the burgers and his smile gets bigger.

"Oh, hey, wow. Thanks, man. With!" His hands are shaking as he takes the burger with onions.

"Pepsi or Dew?" I ask him.

"I love me a Dew."

There is no place to sit, so we hunch down on the sidewalk with our backs against the wall of a liquor store.

"Love me a Pete's," Knob says. He takes an enormous bite; juices run down his beard. I try a smaller bite. It's not a normal burger. The bun is totally soggy, and the first bite seems wrong—soft, bland . . . and completely delicious. I can't stop eating because there's no place to set it down. Knob finishes his in about thirty seconds. Mine doesn't take much longer. By the time I'm done, my hands are all greasy and I've dribbled ketchup down the front of my shirt.

"That hit the spot!" Knob says. He guzzles his Dew. "You find your gal?"

"Not yet."

"You keep looking."

I glance down toward the coffee shop, then at the hamburger line. I'm still hungry.

"You want another one?" I ask. I want to try one with the onions.

"You buying?"

"Sure."

Knob and I cross the street and get in line. We're behind a couple who look about my age. The guy is wearing a Packers cap, a green-and-yellow baseball jacket, and cargo shorts. The girl has hoop earrings, a blond ponytail, and a maroon T-shirt.

"We should've gone to Culver's," the guy is saying. "You don't have to stand in line for an hour, and we could get fries."

"I don't want fries," the girl says.

"Well, I do."

"You're such an ass. You said we could go wherever I wanted."

"I didn't know you were gonna pick Pete's."

"The burgers are pretty good," I say, mostly to stop their arguing. They both turn and look at me, then at Knob. The guy has little eyes that make his face look big, and the girl has a big face that makes her eyes look small. When she looks at Knob, her nose wrinkles, her mouth contorts, and she edges back.

"The line moves fast once it gets going," I say.

"We *live* here," the girl says. Her shirt is printed with the word "Blackhawks"—the Prairie du Chien High School mascot.

"So I guess you know about the no-cheese thing?"

"Gawd," she says, with an eye roll.

"We've eaten here, like, a thousand times," the guy says. His jacket is unbuttoned to show off his Packers T-shirt.

"Do you know Maeve Samms?" I ask.

Knob asks, "That your gal?"

"No."

"She's *new*," the girl says, as if that's the worst possible thing to be.

"Do you know where she lives?"

"Some farm," the guy says.

"Last week she came to school with *straw* in her hair," the girl says with a flip of her straw-colored ponytail. They turn away from us. The guy whispers something; the girl giggles. I look down the street toward the coffee shop and watch a woman cross the street and go in. She is not Gaia. I wonder what it's like for Gaia to go to a new school with kids like these. I wonder if she wears her makeup, her boots and black jeans, her art T-shirts.

"What about Gaia Nygren?" I ask. "Do you know her?"

The girl makes a face. "That freak?" She sniffs and turns her back. I guess Gaia has made an impression on the locals.

The girl whispers something to the guy. He looks back at Knob and says, "Culver's smells better too." They abandon the line and walk away, presumably in the direction of Culver's.

"I don't think they liked me," Knob says.

"I don't think they liked either of us." The line shuffles forward, and suddenly I'm not hungry anymore. Part of it is the greasy burger roiling around in my stomach, but mostly I feel sick about the two petty, nasty locals. I want to chase after them and yell at them for their assholery, but I know it wouldn't do any good.

I take a bill from my wallet and hand it to Knob.

"What's this?" he says.

"I have to go, Knob." I step out of line.

"You want with or without?"

"Neither. It's all yours."

"This is too much, man," he says, looking at the money. I thought I was giving him a ten, but now I see that it's the hundred-dollar bill I got from Bran's mother. My hand starts to reach for it; then I stop.

"Keep it," I hear myself say. "Catch a bus to Rhinelander."

He stares at me, uncomprehending. "Uh . . . thanks?"

"It's cool." I walk down to the coffee shop and look in the window. No Maeve; no Gaia. What if she never shows up? What makes me think she will? She probably has a hundred other things to do on a Saturday afternoon. Feeding the chickens or whatever they do on a farm. She could be having fun.

It hits me like a knee to my balls just how pathetic I am. I try to think of people who are more pathetic. All the losers I've met, and I can't think of one more pathetic than me. Knob? Knob is an okay guy, except for his aroma. And he's *happy*. The huge guy in Hannibal complaining about the lack of golf carts? He was overweight and uncomfortable, but at least he was getting out and doing things, like looking at Tom Sawyer's fence. He told me I had no romance, and maybe he was right, or at least I didn't have as much romance as he did.

Bran? Bran was a jerk, but he'd be fine in his big house with his marble statue of a mother. Even the couple I just left in line. They were nasty, rude, small-eyed small-town snobs, but they had each other. What do I have? Bran Fetzig's hoodie, a John Deere cap, and a ketchup-stained polo shirt that was my dad's.

Maybe the last thing on earth Gaia wants or needs is to see me. Maybe she had a perfectly good reason to dump me. Maybe the barista was right about me being a stalker.

I look back at all the people lining up for their

cheeseless, boiled, pulverized cow muscle, *with* or *without*. Knob is at the front of the line. I wonder how many burgers he'll eat. I can taste the grease coating the back of my throat, and I wish I could throw up. Throw up so hard that I'd turn inside out and disappear. My feet move me down the sidewalk away from the smell of onion and meat and coffee. I only make it a few yards before I sit down on a metal bench in front of a bar called Fort Mulligan's. A mulligan is a do over. My dad used to say it all the time when he screwed up, like when he put a new faucet on the kitchen sink and turned it on and water shot out everywhere. "Guess I better take a mulligan on that," he would say before taking it apart and starting over. I want a mulligan for my whole pathetic life.

I squeeze my eyes shut and take a deep breath through my mouth, let it out shakily. I don't know why I'm feeling this way, like my whole life I've been dealing with assholes and now I have to deal with myself. Was this what it was like for my dad? Like, he thought everything was a crock of shit, and then one day he realized he was the biggest crock of shit of all, so he shot himself on Groundhog Day? Not like the movie. You don't get a mulligan after you shoot yourself in the neck.

Thinking back over the past week—has it only been a week? What did I think I was doing? Where would I end up?

I always knew there was a place where I *could* end

up. Back in Saint Andrew Valley, living with my mom.
Sure, I can drive around pretending to be free, pretending I'm leaving it all behind, but I'm not really free
at all, and I'm not leaving anything behind because
it's all permanently attached to me. Knob was right.
I'm a nexus, and everybody I ever knew or will ever
know is part of me whether I want them to be or not.

Was that why Dad did it? Because it was the only
way he could break free? Am I thinking about him
because I'm sitting on a metal bench?

I open my eyes. There is no river, just a small-town
street on a Saturday afternoon. There is something in
my hand. The Pepsi can. I take a sip; it's warm and
flat. I look around for a trash can. There's a girl with
flame-red hair and a green flannel shirt standing a
few yards away, looking straight at me.

"Stiggy," she says.

It's Gaia.

# Happy Birthday, Ronny

**January 31, two days before Groundhog Day,** was Dad's last birthday.

For the previous several weeks, ever since the holidays, things had been tense and weirdly quiet at home. Every day after work Dad would shut himself in the den until it was time for dinner. He would eat without saying much except for things like, "I don't know why we always have to have salad," or, "This pork has no taste! Factory farms! What a crock!"

Instead of snapping back at him or arguing, Mom would let it pass. That wasn't like her. When Dad was done eating, he'd go back to the den, close the door, and turn on the TV, not even offering to help with the dishes.

Mom took on a bunch of household tasks she'd been putting off. Organizing closets and cleaning under the sink and dusting places that never got dusted. Like she had to keep moving, making our house a better place in every little way she could imagine. I spent a lot of time rereading my comics and Star Wars books.

I didn't get what was going on. I figured it was just winter blahs.

On Dad's birthday everything changed. It was like the sun came out. He announced that he was taking a day off from work and I was taking a day off from school. He took Mom and me out to breakfast at the Saint Andrew Inn. We sat at a window table looking out over the river. I had waffles, bacon, a cinnamon roll, toast, and fresh-squeezed orange juice. They had these miniature jars with four different kinds of jelly and jam, and I tried them all. Mom ordered a spinach omelet and a fresh fruit plate. Dad had eggs Benedict, sausage, pancakes, hash browns, and a Bloody Mary. He wasn't much of a drinker—maybe a beer or two on weekends, and that was it. I guess it was a special occasion.

"Do you remember the last time we came here?" he asked me.

I didn't.

"I'm not surprised—you were only three years old. It was our tenth anniversary."

"We were almost asked to leave," Mom said with a smile.

"What did you do?" I asked.

Dad laughed. "It was what *you* did, Stig."

"You threw a pancake," Mom said. "It hit one of the other diners in the face."

"It was a perfect shot," Dad said. "I figured you'd grow up to be a professional Frisbee player." He reached over and put his hand on my shoulder and squeezed. "But whatever you decide to do with your life, I want you to know we're proud of you."

It was a strange moment. Dad was not a touchy-feely kind of guy, and I don't think he'd ever told me he was proud of me before. I sat there, stunned, my mouth hanging open, with my dad's hand on my shoulder and my mom smiling in a way I hadn't seen in a while. After a few seconds his hand slid away and he started talking about the first time he had ordered eggs Benedict.

"I was about your age, Stig. This girl I was dating invited me out for a fancy brunch with her family. The girl's father ordered eggs Benedict, so I ordered the same thing. I didn't know eggs Benedict from Egg McMuffin. When the waiter brought it, I was completely grossed out by the yellow sauce. I scraped it off. The poached egg was staring up at me like a blobby eye, so I scraped that off too and just ate the ham and the muffin. Then I realized they were all looking at me—the girl, her mom and dad, and her little sister—like I was this unedu-cated Neanderthal." He laughed. "Not far off the mark. Anyway, the girl broke up with me a few days later, and I decided I was going to learn to love eggs Benedict."

Mom said, "On our first date you ordered it for dinner."

"Now you know why. I wanted to make sure you knew I was a sophisticate."

They both thought that was hilarious.

Later that day Mom made Dad's favorite dinner: pot roast with rutabagas and little potatoes. His birthday was the only day of the year we ate rutabagas—Dad called them "swedes"—because neither Mom nor I liked them. While she was cooking, Dad took me to see a matinee at the Heights, that old theater where they showed classic movies. The movie was called *Five Easy Pieces*.

"My all-time favorite film," he said as we settled in.

The movie was kind of slow except for this one part where Jack Nicholson has a fight with a waitress and ends up knocking everything off the table onto the floor. I could imagine doing that. I kept looking at Dad. He was watching the screen so intently, it was like he was inside the movie. I didn't understand a lot of it, especially the ending, but afterward the movie stayed with me.

On the way out of the theater, Dad was quiet. He didn't ask me what I thought about the movie. When we got in the car, I asked him about the ending, where Jack Nicholson gives his girlfriend his wallet and jumps in a truck and leaves her. He thought for a moment before answering.

"It's about not wanting to hurt people," he said. "It's

about keeping all the hurt inside. Bobby just couldn't stand who he was anymore." "Bobby" was the name of Jack Nicholson's character. "He didn't want his misery to spill over onto everybody else."

"Oh," I said, as if I understood.

He gave me a light sock on the shoulder. "Don't be like Bobby," he said, then laughed.

Dad didn't talk much at dinner that night, except to tell Mom how perfect the pot roast was, and how rutabagas were the perfect vegetable. He didn't seem sad, exactly, just very relaxed, like everything was going to be okay. It was the first night in a long time when he didn't once complain about his job, or tell us that some politician was a crock, or how much his back hurt from sitting at a desk all day. Instead he smiled and enjoyed his birthday dinner.

I understand now. He was at peace because that was the day he decided to kill himself.

# "This Is Not a Love Song"
## Public Image Ltd.
### 4:12

**"Naomi told me you were here."**

It takes a second for me to remember that "Naomi" is the name of the barista in the coffee shop.

I say, "Oh. Her. I, um, I was hoping I'd run into you."

"Are you okay, Stiggy?"

"Sure."

"Because you look kind of rough."

"It's been a long week."

"Why did you come here, Stiggy?"

Why? It's a simple question, but I'm having trouble getting the right words out, so I say something else.

"You're wearing a green shirt."

"So?"

"Your hair is red."

"Yeah, and Maeve's hair is green now. Everybody hates us. What are you *doing* here?"

I can't figure out her expression. She doesn't seem *glad* to see me, but she doesn't seem mad or disgusted or anything. Maybe just curious?

"Can we go for a walk?" I hold my breath.

"We can go to the park," she says.

Saint Feriole Island park is a few blocks away, along the river. It's one of those historic sites with lots of old buildings. Some are brick, some are log cabins. There's a museum and a historic villa and a baseball field. People are walking and biking on the narrow road-ways. We walk to the river, neither of us talking, and stand side by side at the railing on the concrete pier. There are two guys fishing from an aluminum boat about a hundred feet offshore. It looks like a father and his young son. It makes me think of my dad.

"Prairie started here, as a fur trading center," Gaia tells me. "It's the second-oldest city in Wisconsin."

"What's the oldest?"

"I don't know. I just know about Prairie because I work here."

"Where do you work?"

"Here, in the park. At the museum gift shop." She points off to the right. "I was working when Naomi called me."

"She acted like she didn't really know you."

"She thought maybe I didn't want to see you."

"Oh." *Do you?* I'm afraid to ask. "I'm not stalking you."

"I didn't think you were."

"I'm just trying to . . . trying to figure things out. Figure out what happened. You know. With us."

Gaia doesn't say anything for a long time. She's not looking at me; she's watching the father and son fishing. Or maybe she's not even seeing them.

"I want to understand," I say.

Gaia nods. "You seem different."

I don't know if that's good or bad, but I ask her, "How so?"

"You haven't said anything bad about anybody."

I think about the arguing couple in line at Pete's, and about Bran, and Allie and Randy, and the tweakers, Babe and Honeypie. I think about Garf.

"I gave my Darth Vader stuff to Garf."

She looks at me for the first time since we got to the river. "You did? What about Wonder Woman?"

"I sold her. To Garf. Only I think he's mad at me right now. We kind of had a fight."

"What did you do?"

I shrug.

She shakes her head and turns back to the river. "Your mom was here."

"She was?" I'm not sure I heard her right.

"Three days ago. I guess my dad told her where I was. She came down with your uncle Donny. She's worried about you."

"She is?"I don't know why that surprises me so much.

"She's your *mom*!" A flash of anger.

A sick pit of guilt and shame opens up in my gut. I've hardly been thinking about Mom at all, telling myself she was probably glad I was gone.

"I guess I should have left a note or something," I mumble.

"You *think*?"

The last time I saw my mom, the morning I left, she had made me pancakes for breakfast. She was getting ready for her Zumba class. She looked so tired, like she was forcing her body to go through the motions, and all I could think about was whether she would notice that her Visa card was missing from her purse.

I can't stand to think about it, so I blurt out the question I came to ask.

"How come you ghosted me?" I ask, and then hold my breath.

Gaia doesn't answer right away. She doesn't answer until I'm about to die of asphyxiation. The kid in the boat has hooked on to a fish; his dad scoops it up with a net. It's about six inches long.

"I missed my period," Gaia says.

I let out my breath, and for a fraction of a second, I think she's referring to a *class* period. Then I think she means "missed" like missing somebody. Then I realize what she is saying.

"When?" I ask, which is sort of irrelevant. Or maybe not.

"In July," she says.

It takes a second for me to get what she said. It's a very long second.

"You're pregnant?"

"I *thought* I was pregnant."

"You're not pregnant?"

"No."

"Did you—"

"Have an abortion? No. My period was late, is all. That happens sometimes. I think I was stressed out. But for a whole month I *thought* I was pregnant."

"Why didn't you tell me?"

"I didn't tell *anybody*. Not even Maeve. I was trying to figure out what to do. And I was thinking about us. I mean, you said you didn't want to be a dad, and I'm only sixteen, and what were we *doing*, anyway? Why did you want to go out with me? I mean, at first?"

I think back to the first time we spoke, at the McDonald's across from school.

"I think it was your shirt."

"*Life Sucks and Then You Die*? I only wore it that once."

"Yeah, but you were wearing it that day."

"So you decided you wanted to go out with me because I was wearing a depressing, nihilistic T-shirt?"

"Nihilistic fashions turn me on." That was supposed to be funny. She is not amused. I guess I don't know what "nihilistic" means.

"So you just thought it would be a good idea to hang out with another depressive?"

"I'm not depressed," I say.

"Really? Your dad committed suicide nine months ago. How are you not depressed?"

"I'm not like my dad."

"I'm not like my mom, either, but that doesn't mean it didn't mess me up when she left."

"Wasn't that, like, a year ago?"

"It was, like, *yesterday*!" Her eyes flash. "It will *always* be yesterday. Do you think you'll forget about *your* dad in a year from now?"

"I guess not." *Life sucks and then you die.*

"I don't think we're good for each other. I mean, getting fake-pregnant, that made me realize, you know?"

"You decided to dump me because you got fake-pregnant?"

"No! I mean, it made me think. It's not just you and me and everything sucks. We were tied up in a miserable, painful little knot: you lost your dad, I lost my mom, and everything sucked."

"Everything?" My voice cracks, and my face and hands feel all prickly. I can't seem to breathe right.

Her face softens. I feel a kernel of hope growing in my chest; then her eyes go crisp.

"I got my period up at the lake, when I was there with my dad and Derek. I'd been thinking I was pregnant, and then all of a sudden I wasn't. The weird thing was, I was kind of disappointed, you know?"

I don't know.

"Not because I *wanted* to be pregnant, but because it took away my choice. You know?"

I still don't know.

"I'd been thinking about it so hard—harder than I've ever thought about anything else. Do I have a kid and be this teen mom? Do I give it away? Do I have an abortion? I still don't know what I'd have done. I'll never know. And that pissed me off. Because that choice was taken away from me."

"I guess, in a way, it was lucky," I say.

"Lucky?" She slams her palms into my chest, nearly knocking me over. "You are stupid, stupid, *stupid*! *Lucky?* You don't get it at all."

"I know, but . . ." But *what*? I'm floundering.

"That's why I had to go," she says in a flat voice, then looks away.

"Because I don't *get* it?"

"Because *I* don't get it, and I just couldn't go back to the way we were. I had to leave. You know?"

I know about leaving.

"And Maeve was down here, and her uncle said I could move in, and I thought if I just left, I could find some space. I could figure out what I wanted, you know? Like Michael is trying to do. Like Maeve."

*Like Stiggy*, I think.

"So your dad just said you could leave?"

"He knew I was having a hard time. He didn't know why, but he's cool that way. He thought it might be good for me. He drove me down here and talked to Maeve's uncle—you know, just to make sure it wasn't some weirdo cult compound or something. It's not. It's nice. I'm going to finish the school year here. Next year I don't know. I might graduate early and go to college someplace where nobody knows me. I've been talking to my mom. I might go to Santa Fe and stay with her."

"I thought you were mad at her."

"She's my *mom*."

Seconds tick by.

"Are you seeing somebody else?" I ask.

"You are such an asshole," she says, without much heat in it.

"I know," I say.

She shakes her head, takes out her phone, looks at it. "I have to get back to work."

"I'll walk you."

"No." She looks straight at me, and I get this chilling sensation like I'm looking into the eyes of a stranger, seeing her for the first time. "Go home, Stiggy. Let your mom know you're okay. Make up with Garf. Make some friends. Be nice." She takes my hand, squeezes it, lets go. "Maybe I'll see you around sometime. Okay?"

I watch her walk away. Black boots, black jeans, green shirt, red hair. It's as if she's turning into somebody else from the top down.

"I like your hair!" I call after her. She doesn't look back.

# Wolverine

**"Sometimes I think he's still alive,"** Garf said. That was way back in April, before Gaia. We were hanging out in Garf's room reading his vintage X-Men comics. "I think the door will crash open and Jimmy will be yelling at me to get my mitts off his precious comics." Garf laughed. "He could be a pain sometimes. These were my dad's comics. He gave them to Jimmy, and when Jimmy died, I got them."

Garf didn't mention his brother very often.

"I know what you mean," I said. "When I wake up in the morning, I'm always kind of startled when I realize my dad isn't there."

"It happens less and less often. To me, I mean. For a

while, every day, I'd have to face that he was gone all over again, and it was painful. Now it only happens every now and then. Dr. Missou said that's normal."

"Dr. Missou?"

"This counselor my parents made me go to. Actually, she kind of helped. After Jimmy died, I was pretty messed up. She told me about the stages of grief. The first one is denial—like, you just can't believe what happened, so you pretend it didn't. Then you get mad, then sad, then depressed, and eventually you're okay."

"So are you okay now?"

Garf shrugged. "I'm not as mad as I used to be."

"What stage do you think I'm at?"

"Everybody has different stages. Dr. Missou says some people skip stages, and they don't always go in the same order."

"I think I'm at the *Wolverine* stage," I said. "Except without the Adamantium claws." I flip forward in the comic I'm reading to the part where Magneto rips the Adamantium out of Wolverine.

Garf said, "The pissed-off stage. Sounds about right."

"Do you think about why they did it? My dad? And your brother?"

"All the time."

I took a gulp from my bottle of Coke, but I did it too fast, and some of it bubbled up out of the neck and spilled all over the comic I was reading.

"Oh, crap! I'm sorry!"

Garf took the comic from me and tried to soak up the Coke with his sleeve. It didn't help much.

"I'm really sorry," I said.

"It's okay." He looked sadly at the soggy comic and set it aside. "It's just a comic book. I'll get over it."

# "Through It All"
## Leftover Cuties
## 3:51

**Looking out over the river, I hear the echoes** of Gaia's voice.

*Go home, Stiggy.*

The father and son have drifted downstream; I can still see them. I think about my dad floating down the river with my uncle Donny. They never made it this far south.

*Let your mom know you're okay.*

I look to my right. Gaia is out of sight. I imagine my mother standing there, looking at me. I clench the steel railing, and every bone in my body aches. I wish she was yelling at me, right now. Or anything.

I close my eyes, breathe in, and let go of the railing. I follow it along the pier until it opens onto a narrow beach. I shuffle to the water's edge and let the little waves lap against the toes of my Walmart shoes. I've driven more than a thousand miles, most of it on the Great River Road, and this is the closest I've been to the water.

*Make some friends. Be nice.*

In other words, don't be a dick.

I toe off my shoes and pull off my socks and roll up my jeans. The water is warmer than I expected. I move deeper, until I'm up to my knees, soaking the rolled-up bottoms of my jeans. Sandy muck oozes up between my toes. I think about the water swirling around my calves, how it got there, how some of those molecules came from the beginning of the river in northern Minnesota, some flowed in from the Saint Croix and other rivers, some of it flowed past the steel benches in East River Park.

"Whoa," I say under my breath.

I drive north on the Great River Road. The sun is pounding on my left shoulder. The trees on my right are raining leaves—in another week their limbs will be bare. In another month the river will be frozen.

I never made it to the Gulf of Mexico, but neither did my dad. What did I think I'd find there? Shrimp boats and alligators? More Brans, more Knobs, more Allies? More smiley Daves, more tweakers and strippers, more friendly salesmen who want to brag about their perfect sons?

What I would never find there is my dad.

*Go home, Stiggy.*

Is that what Dad would say?

*Let your mom know you're okay.*

Is she okay? Dad would want to know. He would want *me* to know.

*Make some friends.*

Dad never had a lot of friends. He had his brother and sister, Donny and Roni, who would listen to him gripe. He had me and Mom. He was friendly with our neighbor Devon—they'd help each other out with things like putting up a shed or fixing a broken lawn mower. Was that it? There was Kenny Oldes, a guy he knew from high school. He'd stop by once a year or so and they'd sit in the backyard and have a beer and talk. Afterward Dad would complain that Kenny, who was a loan officer at Wells Fargo, had gotten boring. "We did some crazy stuff back in the day, me and Kenny. But now all he wants to do is talk about his kids."

They were all at his funeral, along with a few people from his work, my grandmother, a bunch of cousins, and some people I didn't know. Maybe he did have a few friends. Maybe if he'd had more friends, he would still be here.

Me, I have *ex*-friends. And Garf, who might be an ex-friend too. The thought makes me jangly and queasy, so I turn up the music. Billie Holiday is singing about autumn in New York. Her voice is sweet and sticky, and it makes me sad even though she's singing about things pretty and hopeful. When the song is over, I play it again.

La Crosse comes and goes. Onalaska, Holmen, Trempealeau, Fountain City. I'm back on the same stretch of road I took going south, but it looks different, more naked, harsher. Alma, Nelson, Pepin. Before, I thought of them like beads on a chain. Now they seem more like fraying knots on a rope. Stockholm, Maiden Rock, Bay City. The sun is barely visible; the river is dark.

I am at the SuperAmerica four blocks from home, standing under harsh fluorescent lamps, pumping gas. A chill wind cuts through the open front of my hoodie. I zip up and tug my cap down and watch the numbers tick over on the pump. A few hours ago I stood at the river with Gaia. It feels like weeks ago that I left town with a wallet full of cash, my mom's credit card, and no destination, but it has only been a few days. I am imagining pulling into the driveway at home, walking up to the door . . . Do I just open it with my key? Or do I knock?

My father's iPod says eight o'clock. I wonder what Garf is doing. Selling my junk on eBay? Did he sell Wonder Woman?

Garf's mom answers the door. Like Garf, she's incredibly skinny with the same pointy nose as her son.

"Hello, Steven," she says.

"Hi, Mrs. Neff." I maybe haven't mentioned, but Garf's mom teaches English at Saint Andrew.

"I haven't seen you in school recently." She looks at me closely. "Are you okay?"

People keep asking me that.

"I'm fine. Is Garf around?"

"I don't know about *around*, but he's in his room. Why don't you see if you can extract him?"

Garf's door is open. He is sprawled on his rumpled bed reading a textbook. He kind of jerks when I walk in, then gives me a half-lidded look to show how much he doesn't care.

"Hey," I say.

He grunts. "You're back," he says.

"I'm back." I look around, and find Wonder Woman on the shelf next to BB-8. "You didn't sell her."

"Not yet. I suppose you want her back."

I shake my head.

"What *do* you want?"

"Nothing."

"I gave all your Vader stuff to Geoff."

"Including the TIE fighter he broke?"

Garf nods warily.

"Good," I say. "He'll enjoy them."

Garf sits up and sets his book aside. I can tell he isn't deliriously happy to see me, but he's curious.

"You look like crap," he says.

I nod. I know it's true.

"Your mom was over here looking for you last week.

She thought I might know where you went. Guess what? Didn't know; didn't care."

"I'm sorry if I was a dick," I say.

*"If?"* His eyebrows go up.

"Okay. I'm sorry. I *was* a dick."

"Have you seen your mom?"

"I wanted to see you first." I want to see my mom so bad, it hurts, but I am also afraid. I thought it would be easier to talk to Garf, but he isn't making it easy at all.

"She's worried about you."

"I know."

Garf snorts and grabs a pair of Nike skate shoes. They look new. He slides his feet in without tying them and stands up.

"Let's go outside. You kind of reek."

"Thanks a lot."

"Well, you do."

I follow him down the hall and out the door and along the walkway to the street. He turns right.

"Where are we going?" I ask.

He keeps walking, laces flopping. I fall in beside him.

# Big Ben

**Dad liked to work in the garage. He would** invent things to do there, such as sharpening the hundreds of tiny blades on the chain saw that I had never seen him use. One day last fall I went out there to see what he was doing, and he was doing nothing. Just sitting at his workbench.

"Dad?" I said.

He turned his head slowly and smiled. It was a sad smile. "Stiggy. Hey."

"What are you working on?"

"Nothing. Some things you can't fix. Some things are just broken."

"Like what?"

"This clock." He waved a hand at the old-fashioned

windup alarm clock on the bench. It looked like a cartoon alarm clock, with a big dial and a sort of metal loop on top. "It was my father's. It's called a Big Ben. It was made back in the thirties. They still make them, but the new ones are battery operated. This one you had to wind up every night. The spring is broken. I can't fix it."

"I bet somebody could."

"I like to fix things myself. Besides, it would cost more to have it repaired than it's worth."

"But it was your dad's!"

He stood up and put the clock on a shelf above his bench.

"I thought I could fix it, but I can't."

# "I Try"

## Macy Gray
## 3:57

**"I drove down the Great River Road,"** I say to Garf. "Met some interesting people."

He doesn't say anything. He's walking fast. The wind is behind us, and some leaves are keeping pace.

"I met a stripper in Iowa," I say. "She called herself an *ecdysiast*."

"Same thing," Garf says. He knows words like that.

"I bought drugs for some meth addicts. I robbed a grocery store."

He looks at me. I have his attention.

"Actually, I was the getaway driver. Oh, and my car got stolen in Saint Louis, but I found it in Kansas City."

"That sounds like so much fun that I'm surprised you came back."

"I ran out of money."

We walk a block without talking. He stops and looks up. Thirty feet above us a pair of shoes hangs from a utility line.

"Oh," I say.

Garf says nothing.

"You want me to get them down?"

He crosses his arms. I consider the problem. Throw something at them? Find a really long stick? Call the fire department? I've heard they save kittens from trees. Maybe they save shoes, too.

None of those ideas seems workable.

"I guess I owe you a pair of shoes," I say.

He hits me. I never saw it coming, and if someone had told me it was coming, I would not have believed it. Not from Garf. His bony fist lands right on the tip of my nose, and I fall back on my butt. I'm more startled than hurt, but my nose immediately starts bleeding. I pinch it shut. Garf is standing over me. His fists are bunched at his sides, and his whole body is shaking.

"Give me your shoes," he says. His voice is shaking too. I know I could take him, but I also know I won't try. I almost wish he would hit me again.

I kick off my Walmart specials. Garf grabs them. I watch him walk off down the leaf-littered street. He stops half a block away and ties my sneakers together by the laces and throws them up at a utility wire. It takes him a few tries, but he finally gets it, and now my shoes are where they will stay until the laces rot.

I wait until he is out of sight before I let go of my nose and wipe it on the sleeve of Bran's hoodie. It's not that bad. It wasn't much of a punch.

"Damn, Garf." I'm sort of proud of him.

I stand up. The asphalt radiates cold up through my socks. Leaves tumble and hiss down the street. Chill autumn wind cuts up under the hoodie. The streetlight above me flickers. A few yards away a whirlwind lifts a pile of leaves from the gutter and sucks them up and scatters them. There is a reason why these things keep happening to me—I can feel it swirling around me like the leaves, trying to make a shape but collapsing into chaos before it can form an answer.

I pull my hood up and head off in the opposite direction from Garf, even though it takes me farther away from my car. I walk past leafy lawns and winterized homes, past driveways staked with reedy orange curb markers waiting for snow, past a row of stores— florist, insurance, barber—all closed for the night. I stop and peer in the window of a watch repair shop. A dark, hooded creature stares back at me.

"There you are," I say.

No reply.

I turn away, unzip the hoodie, shrug it off, let it fall to the sidewalk, and walk into the chill wind toward home.

# ACKNOWLEDGMENTS AND CONFESSIONS

Stiggy Gabel, under many an alias, lived inside me for half a century. For a decade I had been trying to coax him out.

"You could be a star," I told him. "I'll write a book about you!"

"Buzz off," he said—or less polite words to that effect.

In the fall of 2016, I ran into Geoff Herbach, the author of *Stupid Fast*, *Hooper*, and several other excellent YA novels. I mentioned Stiggy and a germ of an idea I had about sending him on a solo road trip down the Mississippi River. Geoff, it turned out, was writing a not dissimilar story—not a road trip novel, but a story with characters, settings, and situations that echoed mine. Some of his story would be set in Prairie du Chien, a small Wisconsin town on the Mississippi River. Since Stiggy would be heading in that direction, I suggested that we do a crossover with a few of our characters.*

I went home that day thinking about road trips.

I imagined myself getting behind the wheel of a car and leaving everything behind with no destination, just an open road and no regrets. I pitched the idea to Stiggy. He thought it didn't completely suck.

Coincidentally, I had been invited to deliver a keynote address at the 2017 Fay B. Kaigler Children's Book Festival in Hattiesburg, Mississippi. Airplane tickets had been purchased. As the date neared, it occurred to me that the unwritten road trip novel needed some hands-on-the-wheel research. I called Karen Rowell, the director of the festival. She was completely supportive. The airplane ticket they had paid for was canceled. I set out in my car from Minnesota and headed for Hattiesburg, trying to see the trip downriver through the eyes of Stiggy Gabel.

Meanwhile, in New York City, my editor, David Gale, was wondering why I had not delivered the novel I had promised him several months earlier. I told him I didn't want to write that book anymore. I wanted to do something completely different. I told him about Stiggy. David, a patient, insightful, and above all flexible editor, said, "Okay, I like it, go." Or words to that effect.

Without the encouragement and blessings of Geoff, Karen, and David, *Road Tripped* would never have happened. Thanks, guys!

Thank you also to my friend Jim Mitchell, who helped walk me through Kansas City's suburban sociology. And to Steve Brezenoff for the gaming help.

And to my oldest and still best friend, Rod Folland, whose memory is superior to mine, for helping me remember those limestone caves. We were there, and it was terrifying. And to my brother-in-law Rog Bates for sharing a certain youthful misadventure he had while trying to exchange an item at a Florida department store. I modified it and put it in the book. Rog might reveal more if you catch one of his stand-up acts.

Last, but never least, my thanks and love to Mary Logue—my partner, my first reader, and my first editor—for her wise words and understanding. The title was her idea.

*Which characters appear in both books? In the end, Geoff and I took our stories in unexpected directions—but we still have Prairie du Chien in common.*